CREATURE

A HORROR NOVEL

FLINT MAXWELL

Copyright © 2022 by Flint Maxwell

Cover Design © 2022 by Carmen DeVeau

Edited by Sonya Bateman

Special thanks to Sabrina Roote

All rights reserved. No portion of this book may be reproduced in any form without permission from the publisher, except as permitted by U.S. copyright law. For permissions email: fm@flintmaxwell.com

This is a work of fiction. Names, characters, places, and incidents either are the products of the author's imagination or are used fictitiously. Any resemblance to actual persons, living or dead, businesses, companies, events, or locales is entirely coincidental.

The author greatly appreciates you taking the time to read his work.

For Calvin,
Your first, and not your last

Everyone is a moon, and has a dark side which he never shows to anybody.

— MARK TWAIN, *FOLLOWING THE EQUATOR*

BEFORE
THE THING IN THE WOODS

OCTOBER 3, *2008*

Illuminated by a full moon, Owen Carver—eighteen and a little buzzed—thinks he sees a shadow pass between the trees in front of him.

He is standing in a field near a collection of vacant factory buildings, staring into what seems like the infinite darkness of the surrounding woods. He is not alone; two others are with him: Ryan Kensington and Dave Rivers.

Officially, these woods are nameless, but the younger residents of Pickwick, Ohio, have taken to calling them *The Hollow*.

Because they are empty inside, almost completely devoid of life.

Trees stay dead year-round, shrubs sprout only the slightest bit of green in the spring, and no matter the time of day, you will hear no insects buzzing or birds chirping.

But…if you listen very closely on windless nights, you *might* hear a voice—just the faintest whisper of syllables.

They say this voice belongs to a witch.

The Hollow Witch.

———

Ryan and Dave had told Owen the story of the legend and the Blood Rock an hour or so earlier as they rode around town, guzzling beer and sipping from a bottle of cheap vodka that Ryan had stolen from the gas station.

Owen had thought it was all bogus. He laughed it off.

"It's real," Dave said from the front seat. He was a big guy, even bigger than Owen, who stood a few inches over six feet and was two hundred pounds of lithe, athletic muscle. "People go missing 'round here all the time."

Owen leaned forward and wiggled his fingers. "*Oooo!* You're telling me you *actually* believe it was a witch?" He glanced at the six-pack sitting next to him in the backseat and reached for another beer. Truth be told, the talk of witches and curses and missing people unsettled him. "That's stupid."

"Nah, bro, it's not stupid!" Dave said. "She takes these people, guts them and then uses their organs for potions that help her live forever. I mean, dude, there's so many dead people back there, the leaves don't grow on the trees no more!"

"Or…you know…maybe it was all the chemicals from the factories?" Owen said.

But tonight wasn't a night for logic.

From the driver's seat, Ryan's gaze flicked to the rearview and he looked at Owen. "If you think it's so stupid, New Kid, why don't we drive out to the factories and you see for yourself?" he said.

Owen wasn't afraid of anything. In his almost eighteen years on this earth, he had never met a feat he couldn't accomplish. He hadn't answered immediately, though, instead turning to the window and watching the dark trees pass by in a blur.

"Well, Carver?" Ryan said.

Owen faced the front and reached a hand

between the seats. "Fine. But gimme some of that vodka."

And here Owen is, still staring into The Hollow, replaying the movement he thinks he has seen deep in the abyss before him. His bravery is fleeting. A coldness has begun to spread inside his chest, digging down into his ribs like roots.

"Hey, fat boy, don't drink it all!" Ryan says from behind, snapping Owen out of his own head.

"No-no-no, I'm cuttin' you off, bro," Dave says. "You're already hammered."

"Whatever, I'll just go steal more. You know…'cause *I'm* not too chickenshit to do it."

Owen turns around as the plastic vodka bottle hits the ground. Around eight that evening, he had waited outside of the Gas 'N Go while Ryan and Dave went in and purchased a bag of Doritos and some Vanilla Coke. All a ploy, of course. The real merchandise had been stuffed into Ryan's cargo pants: an eleven-dollar bottle of Sobieski that tastes like rubbing alcohol to go along with the six-pack of Bud Light that Dave procured from his dad's mini-fridge.

"There ya go," Dave says now, wiping his mouth with the back of his hand. "Drink up, then, Ry, but just remember I'm not gonna be the one carrying your dumbass home when you're too drunk to stand. You'll be crawling."

With a sneer, Ryan bends and snatches the vodka from its spot in the tall grass. He twists off the lid, holds up the middle finger of his left hand, and downs a few more hearty gulps. "Ahhh," he says, grimacing from the vodka's burn. "I don't need some chickenshit carrying me around anyway, Fatty."

Dave is unbothered by Ryan's remarks, but Owen cringes anytime the big senior's weight is brought up. It makes him think of the kids who teased his little brother, John, back in Pennsylvania. While John isn't overweight, he *is* a little on the nerdy side. They could be ruthless. Owen wonders why everyone can't just get along.

Hearing Ryan say these things to Dave also rubs him the wrong way. He likes Ryan. He's a natural leader and for the most part kind. Not to mention, he can pass the rock like Steve Nash. That's always a plus. Back at Corbin High, Owen had to fight three defenders just to get his shot off, but Ryan makes it so much easier. He has this game sense on the court Owen has never seen before. He can tell when and what a defender will do on nearly every possession. To keep that synergy on the court, Owen believes they have to get along *off* the court too.

A sudden chant breaks out.

"New Kid! New Kid!"

Owen turns and chuckles.

"Well, are you gonna do it or not, pussy?" Ryan barks.

"Fuck off. Don't call me that."

A sloppy grin spreads across Ryan's face. "Oh, sorry...I meant, *chickenshit.*"

The first step is the hardest, but with the vodka and beer making Owen's head swim with false courage, he's able to push past the mental block and step through some bramble. Another step. Dry twigs snap beneath his Converse, the sound almost deafening in the stillness of the night. Now both of his feet are in the woods. He turns and looks back. Dave is wide-eyed, his sunburned face as white as the full moon above; but Ryan is still smiling as he makes a shooing motion with his left hand.

Ignoring the tremors rippling through his arms and legs, Owen grits his teeth and plunges deeper into the woods. He has gone fifteen steps—yes, he is counting—and looks again. Disorientation sweeps over him, because he can no longer see the field. The woods seem to have constricted around him, the dark, jagged branches reaching out, crossing over each other.

Owen turns to the right and thinks he must've looked the wrong way, but all he sees is more trees and more branches. His throat tightens. It is becoming harder to breathe. He scratches at his Adam's apple and tries to swallow. His mouth feels like it is coated in sandpaper.

He turns the other way.

The trees are moving, he thinks, and he's not bothered by how silly that sounds. In fact, he finds it downright terrifying.

Owen backs up, head on a swivel, eyes darting from tree trunk to tree trunk. "Guys?" he says. "Yo?"

Faintly, Ryan's voice drifts into the woods. "Are you at the Rock yet? I don't hear you calling her name!"

He sounds far away. Thousands of feet. Miles, even.

"I don't—" Owen begins before he trips over something he can't see, a root or a rock, and he falls on the soggy forest floor. The breath is knocked out of him. He takes a moment to collect himself, thinking, *You're fine. It's just a regular forest. There's no witch. There's nothing…*

The thought fades. He stares down at his right hand, which is planted in the dirt. Beneath his palm, the ground pulses rhythmically as if it is breathing. Owen bites down a scream and climbs to his feet. If he had been buzzed-going-on-drunk before, he was stone-cold sober now.

"Owen?" Dave shouts, but the sound is dampened. It is almost like Owen has sunk to the bottom of a pool and Dave is speaking to him from dry land.

I gotta just get it over with, he thinks as he blinks a few times and stares at the ground where his hand was a minute ago. Owen lets a nervous chuckle free. It's relieving. He shakes his arms and jumps from foot to foot, like a boxer getting loose before a big fight. He feels better, and his head is a bit clearer.

"I got this," he whispers. "No big deal."

The Blood Rock should be in front of him soon. Dave said he wouldn't be able to miss it. It's the size of a car and covered in graffiti.

Walking carefully for another thirty or so seconds, Owen finally spots it. It is marred by carvings and spray paint. Crudely drawn penises, skulls, swastikas, and hearts with names and initials inside of them. All of it is ugly, but it brings him comfort, because it means others have been here. By the looks of it, *a lot* of others.

When he is closer, two words catch Owen's eye. Near the top of the rock, half obscured by the third six in a deeply etched *666,* are the words *SHE WATCHES.*

They are written in what looks like blood.

For a brief moment, Owen suddenly feels as helpless as a little boy again.

"Shit," he whispers, shaking his head as he steps toward the big rock and puts his hand over a deep gash. He clears his throat and says as loudly as he can, "HOLLOW WITCH!"

There's one time; two more to go.

"HOLLOW WITCH!"

Twice.

His lips part, preparing to form the *H* for the third time: "*Hah*—"

He sees movement out of the corner of his eye, and the words die in his throat.

Owen whirls around, half-expecting to see nothing at all. But this is not the case. There is something there, all right. It passes between the trees deeper in the forest. A large, hunched-over figure.

"What the hell…?" he whispers.

"That's two!" Ryan shouts from the fields. "Don't wuss on us, New Kid!"

Owen's frozen brain kicks into gear. He realizes what this is now. It's not an initiation; it's a prank.

"All right, assholes," he says, standing straighter and speaking louder. "You're hilarious, but I can tell that's you, Dave!"

He squints. The figure is still there in the distance, wading in a pool of shadows.

Owen turns to where he thinks he has come from and shouts, "For real, guys! Joke's over! Help me get outta here, I don't wanna get lost!"

When he turns back, he sees the figure has advanced.

"What?" Dave shouts, but the voice comes from far behind him, not from where this figure waits. "You okay, dude?"

An alarm blares in Owen's head. Years of evolutionary warnings going off like a tornado siren. Standing upright, the figure is partially illuminated by the full moon. Light gleams in its eyes. They are a violent red dotted with small yellow pupils. Inhuman, yet the thing stands like a man.

It comes farther into the light, hunching over again—or rather crouching like a sprinter on the starter block. The figure has a snout, long and ridged, and a mouth full of fangs. Its arms hang past its knees, its fingers claw-like, its body covered in gray fur and bloody gashes.

This is not Dave. It cannot be.

This isn't happening—this isn't real—there's no way in hell…

Perhaps it is a different friend of Ryan and Dave's. Bobby Welton in a monster suit from the Halloween U.S.A. store, maybe?

But Owen can't fully buy that idea, because he has started to think it's not a person at all. He has started to think it's a creature, something that shouldn't exist in the real world. Something that somehow does.

And now the creature growls. It is a terrible sound, a *hungry* sound, that rumbles from inside the thing's chest.

Owen's knees give out on him. He takes another hard seat on the forest floor. Loose rocks stab his tailbone and the backs of his thighs, filling him with pain he is too frightened to acknowledge.

As the creature hunches back over, its face disappearing into the shadows, something like a gasp mixed with a scream squeaks from Owen's throat.

I have to be hallucinating, he thinks. *I have to be.* He squeezes his eyes shut, hoping it'll be gone when he opens them.

Please be a tree, please just be a tree, please don't be real.

Squinting now and—

Relief barrels into his gut like a sucker punch.

See? You're losing your mind, he tells himself, because there is nothing there in front of him, no giant creature with red eyes and dripping fangs, no Hollow Witch. Only the still woods. Creepy in their own right, but not dangerous.

Owen has no intention of finishing the dare. He pivots and heads back toward the field where Ryan and Dave's voices have come from.

"Hey! Where you guys at?"

He waits a moment, standing in a small clearing he doesn't remember, the pale moonlight shining down on his shoulders.

The others give no answer. All he hears now is the wind. There aren't even the sounds of bugs or birds or forest critters. He must've taken a wrong turn somewhere.

Shit.

He wishes John would've tagged along with him

tonight. For a kid who likes to stay in and watch nerdy movies and play video games, Owen's little brother is surprisingly smart when it comes to navigating the wilderness. Probably because John is smart in general.

They used to play *Jeopardy!* when they were boys, tallying a point for each correct answer on a small dry erase board. Being a few years older, Owen always thought he'd win no problem, but once John got the hang of the game's format, he would say the answer before Alex Trebek was finished reading the question. Owen never stood a chance. His little brother was damn smart. He'd be able to get them out of these woods.

God, Owen would do just about anything to be back home sitting on the couch with his little bro, playing *Jeopardy!* or watching *Star Wars* together for the millionth time.

Soon, he tells himself and calls out for the others again. But as if in response to his voice, another sound joins in with the blowing wind.

A low grumble.

Slowly, Owen turns toward it, and on the opposite side of the clearing he sees the same violent red eyes from earlier.

"No," he moans. "You're not real."

Without thinking, he turns back around and runs into the bramble. He doesn't care if he's going the wrong way, because the right way is any direction away from that *thing*.

He gets about a dozen steps before the vines and branches start to slap at him. The pricker bushes jab into his flesh, whack his face, slice his cheeks and brow.

Owen, grunting, ignores the pain and forces himself to keep going.

Don't look back, he thinks. *Don't look back, don't look back, don't look back—*

But even when we tell ourselves not to look back, we never listen, do we?

Owen does look back and there's—

A sound like a chainsaw fills the void of the woods.

He stumbles as the dark figure launches at him. It is so large it eclipses the swollen moon above and becomes this backlit silhouette of fur and muscle and claws.

Owen is still screaming as the creature sinks its teeth into his throat.

CHAPTER 1
WELCOME TO PICKWICK

THE SUMMER of '09 was a summer of firsts for me.

During that time, I made my first *real* best friend, I had my first *real* crush, and I learned how to fend for myself…but it wasn't all good things.

It was my first summer as an only child. And it was the summer I would come face-to-face with a monster (or *monsters,* depending on how you view Ziggy).

Back then, I found out there was a lot more to the world than what our eyes could see. A lot more *terrible* things.

My name is John Carver.

And the summer of '09 was the summer I grew up.

This story actually begins in the fall of 2008, a few months after my mother, my older brother Owen, and myself moved from Corbin, Pennsylvania, to Pickwick, Ohio.

It begins on a Friday in early October. That was when Owen went missing.

He had come to me that evening and asked if I wanted to go out with him and some of his new friends. They were going to ride around town, maybe hit the Walmart in Stone Park and mess around on the bikes in the toy section, or head to the automotive side and climb into the big tires and push each other down the aisles until they inevitably got kicked out.

Owen was just being polite. For lack of a better term, I was a hermit. Leaving my house (my *shell*) for fun scared me. I barely did it in Corbin and hadn't even attempted to do it since arriving in Pickwick.

Friends didn't come easy for me like they did for Owen. I swear the guy could've made a pal out of Darth Vader if the two ever crossed paths.

Owen would walk into a room, flash his

winning smile, and everyone there would be eating out of the palm of his hand a minute or two later.

Thing is, Owen didn't even know he had this effect on people. Most guys, I think, would abuse that power. They'd use it to get what they wanted, take advantage of any who fell under their spell, and try to get to the top of the social food chain.

Not Owen. He was just…being *Owen*.

I told him as fun as all that sounded, I couldn't. Even if I wanted to, I would've still said no.

One of the guys Owen was hanging with that night was this jerk named Ryan Kensington.

He was the big man on campus at Pickwick High, the stereotypical *jock-hole*. My first day at the new school, Ryan knocked my books out of my hands and said, "Watch it, New Kid."

I never told Owen on account of him and Ryan getting along so well. They were both going to be stars that coming basketball season. Why bother, you know?

Ryan left me alone after he found out I was Owen's younger brother anyway, and that's all I wanted—to be left alone, especially by people like him.

"C'mon, John," Owen said, standing in my bedroom doorway. "It'll be fun. Ryan's gonna get us"—he glanced over his shoulder to make sure our mother was nowhere around (she was working, she almost always was, but Owen and me both knew she had supersonic hearing), and tilted an imaginary bottle back, making a guttural glugging sound—"some...*you know...*"

I faked a gag. Ryan was going to get some beer and maybe some liquor, and I hated the taste of both more than I hated the smell. I was more of a Sunkist Orange and yellow Gatorade kind of guy.

"Johnny-Boy...don't be like that. Come out with the fellas, have some fun, make some friends. *Live a little!*"

I rolled my eyes, mostly at him calling me Johnny-Boy. I was not a fan of that nickname.

I was sitting at the little desk in my tiny closet of a bedroom. An English textbook was splayed out, open to an Edgar Allan Poe story I was supposed to answer three critical thinking questions about, but I hadn't been reading it. Not really. I tried, believe me, but my eyes were jumping over the words and not taking anything in.

"I got home—"

"Homework?" Owen finished. "Yeah, right. I know as soon as I leave this room, you're gonna hop on the Xbox and play Halo or watch some old movie you've already seen a million times." He sighed. "Man, you're about to be sixteen! It's time to ditch that stuff and start having some fun." He flashed that big grin of his. "And who better to have some fun with than your big bro?"

I almost caved. It was hard not to, but he hadn't been wrong about my plans. It was part of the reason I couldn't focus on my reading.

My mother had finally gotten Time Warner Cable to come out and hook up our internet. We were only able to afford the cheapest tier (*slowest*) speed, but it was better than nothing.

All I wanted to do was slay some Covenant aliens and work on getting my rank up in the Lone Wolves playlist. Then, if the internet bottomed out, as it often did, I'd plop down on the couch and watch a movie or three.

That was my absolute favorite thing to do, watch movies. The magic existed on the silver screen. I would melt into the world of make-believe for a couple hours and all would be right.

"C'mon, little bro," Owen said. "You have to find some friends sooner or later. There's more to life than movies and video games."

"Hey, I do other things."

"Like what?" Owen raised both eyebrows and

stroked the few wiry black hairs he tried to pass off as a mustache.

I looked around my room. "Uh…like…well—"

Since we'd only been here a short while, most of my stuff was still in the moving boxes. My mother thought I hadn't unpacked because of laziness, but the truth was that unpacking would've made the move *official* for me.

I didn't want that. As much as I disliked Pennsylvania and the kids and the teachers, that dreadful place was still home to me. It was familiar.

There, the worst thing that happened was I got beat up a little or got called some dumb names. In Pickwick, although it hadn't happened yet, the possibilities were endless.

Maybe I'm full of crap, I don't know, but there was a bad vibe about this place. It hung in the air like an impending thunderstorm—threatening, brooding, electric.

Owen stepped into the room, pushed an empty backpack off the foot of my bed, and plopped down on the mattress.

The box springs groaned beneath his weight. He was a big guy. Not fat, not skinny, but solid.

He played the power forward position, the same position as legends like Charles Barkley and

Dennis Rodman, but he moved like a point guard, with agility and ball handling skills that were, as the Corbin Express had put it, *"Allen Iverson-esque."*

Yeah, he was big, but Owen was a gentle giant. Still, people never messed with him.

"All you do is game, watch those lame *Space Trek* movies, and—"

"Uh, excuse me?" I said. "It's *Star Wars*, and you know it."

Owen winked. He knew it, all right. He was the one who turned me on to them back when we were little.

I've never felt more excited than I had when I saw Darth Vader for the first time, boarding the Tantive IV via explosion with a legion of Stormtroopers at his side. The laser beams, the smoke, Vader's sleek black armor, and the music—oh man, it didn't get better than that for seven-year-old me.

Except…it kind of did.

After we finished *A New Hope*, Owen had popped *The Empire Strikes Back* into the VCR, and I'm pretty sure I didn't blink for the entire two hours and four minutes it rolled on the screen.

As he got older, Owen drifted away from the so-called nerdy stuff. He got more into the sports and the girls and the fast cars.

As I got older, I didn't. My head stayed in a galaxy far, far away.

"All right," Owen said. "*Star Wars,* my bad. But between that and watching all those Jenna Foxx videos online…"

I buried my face in my hands, my cheeks as red and hot as fire.

"Yeah, yeah," Owen said. "I saw the search history."

I peeked between my fingers at him. Unsurprisingly, he was all smiles. "Did…did Mom see?"

Owen leaned back on his right elbow, the bed protesting his weight, almost sounding like it was ready to give up and collapse. He looked down at his fingernails and studied them, the grin never leaving his face.

"Nah, nah, don't worry about it, man. I cleared it. Put a couple of normal searches in there for good measure. YouTube, MySpace, some NBA and NFL blog sites, the works. If she ever catches on to this computer thing, we might need a better system. But for now, it'll do." He looked at me with wide eyes. "Which is something *you* gotta get better at, man! You want Mom to punt the Dell to the town dump or something? Remember what happened when Hunter left that DVD at the house in Corbin?"

"*Big Butt Backdoor Babes*, yeah, I remember."

Oh boy, did I remember.

"*Big Butt Backdoor Babes* 2, actually," Owen corrected. "But yeah, Mom was ready to call in the whole congregation to perform a pornographic exorcism on us."

That was true. Our mother, God bless her heart, was not a fan of that particular industry.

"She told Pastor Vic the very next Sunday," Owen continued, shaking his head. "He took me aside and said some shit about it being normal to feel Satan tempting us, but I must resist unless I wanted to perish in a lake of fire for all eternity. Scared the shit outta me and got me on a straight path of goodness."

"Well," I said, "that didn't last long."

Owen shrugged. "'Satan's Temptations' would be a good band name, don't you think?" He pushed himself off the bed and stuck out his hand toward me. "You sure you don't wanna tag along? It'd be nice for you to mingle a bit. And it never hurts having upperclassmen as friends." Another winning smile. "Or me as your brother."

"Really, I'm okay."

"All right. Can't force you, nerd," he said, but he said *nerd* lovingly. Not the way some of the kids back in Corbin used to say it. "You gonna leave me hanging?"

"Huh?"

He nodded at his still-outstretched hand. I raised mine to slap him five, but he pulled back.

"On second thought…after seeing what you were doing on the web, maybe not."

"Screw you," I said, and a half-second later, Owen was on me, pulling my head into his arms and grating his knuckles over my scalp. I flailed and laughed and told him to quit it, but it didn't hurt.

He was never the type of big brother who beat on me. We had our scrapes, don't get me wrong, but like I said, he was a gentle giant.

We parted. "All right, man," Owen said. "Study up, remember to clear your browser history, and have a good rest of your night." Then he kissed me atop of my messy hair.

That was the last I ever saw of him.

I remember my mother coming home from work the next day. Like I said earlier, she was always working. She'd do a late shift and then be back at work the next morning.

I was asleep when she came home Friday night and only had been up a couple hours before she had finished her Saturday day shift around two.

She was a bartender at a country club right off Eastgate called the Elk Lodge. It was a nice place, kind of classy, but weirdly strict on who could and couldn't come in.

You had to show your membership at the front door to this guy in a little booth who was always wearing this dumb hat with antlers sticking out of it.

Owen and I called it "Walley World," like the amusement park the Griswolds were trying to get to in that Chevy Chase flick *National Lampoon's Vacation*. It was just pure coincidence that the guy who ran the club was named Walter. As far as we knew, no one called him Walley—not to his face, at least.

My mother got the job before we moved to Ohio. After she followed my father to Pennsylvania, I guess she had kept in touch with this woman named Candice over the years. They both had graduated from Pickwick High back in '91, and it seemed like those good ol' days were all they talked about when they were on the phone together.

Well, my mother, she was already thinking about moving back. Pennsylvania was chock full of bad memories. Long story short, my father cheated, not once but a few times, and then he hightailed it out of the state when I was about fourteen, leaving my mother with two rowdy boys and little money.

Candice had let my mother know the Elk Lodge was looking for another bartender around the same time our landlord said he was raising the rent at our place in Corbin, which my mother couldn't afford.

Since she wanted to go back home anyway, that was that. Goodbye Pennsylvania, hello Ohio.

Luckily, Candice, who volunteered for every Friday night fish fry at the Lodge, put in a good word for my mother, and the job was hers almost instantly. We were packed and on the road not even a month later.

When my mother pulled into the drive on that Saturday in October 2008, I had been on the front porch, sitting in a wicker chair and reading the latest issue of *Empire* magazine, which specialized in behind-the-scenes information on my favorite movie genres—sci-fi and fantasy.

The weather was warmer than it had any right

to be for early fall, and what Owen had said the day before about me not doing anything but jacking off, watching *Star Wars,* and playing *Halo* had sort of gotten under my skin.

Summer had ended, and I had spent a grand total of maybe eight hours in the sun—whenever it was my turn to mow the lawn or help our distant neighbors with yard work. So I had the complexion of a potato grown under a set basement stairs.

Being from Pennsylvania, I knew harsh winters. I knew that when the snow started to fall, all I would want was sunshine.

From what I'd heard, Ohio was even worse during the winter months. So a sudden change of heart had me trying to enjoy the weather while I could.

It wasn't bad sitting out there on the porch, paging through photos and skimming interviews about upcoming movies (apparently the new Bond flick was the bloodiest one yet, and *Twilight,* a vampire love story, was going to take the throne from *Harry Potter* as the best YA book adaptation ever).

People were out and about. Some were walking their dogs; husbands and wives were pushing their kids along in strollers; middle-aged men and women in spandex were jogging; and everyone was smiling and happy.

When someone passed by, they'd raise a hand and say, "Hey, how ya doin'?" or "Soak up that sun while you can, young man!" and I'd always reply with the same practiced "I'm great!" and "I will! You bet!" even though the social anxiety I'd felt was crippling.

What can I say? My mother raised me to be polite.

"One day," my mother said as she climbed the front porch steps, "I'm gonna come home to you reading an actual book."

I closed the magazine. "This is a book."

"Candice is always reading those celebrity gossip rags: *'Britney's Humiliating Betrayal!', 'Angelina Jolie: How She Got Thin Fast!', 'Celebs, They're Just Like Us!'*" My mother shook her head. "I'll tell you the same thing I tell Candice: these magazines are nothing but picture books for adults!"

"For someone who doesn't like the gossip magazines, you sure do know a lot of headlines," I said with a smile.

My mother offered me an exhausted look as she took the *Empire* from my grasp. She examined the cover, and then riffled through the pages. "Vampires in love?"

"I don't know," I said.

"Well, I'll give you this: that Daniel Craig is quite a handsome man, isn't he?"

I snatched the magazine back. "Gross, Mom."

Smirking, she dug out a cigarette from her purse, lit it, brought it to her lips, and inhaled deeply. As she exhaled, she closed her eyes and a cloud of smoke drifted around her head.

She never smoked inside or in the car. Hell, she barely ever did it around us, too worried about second-hand smoke and all that. She must've been stressed to do it now.

The move had not been easy. The house we settled in was another rental a few streets over from where she grew up, and although she wouldn't talk about money with us, I knew from how much she was working that the rent had to be a lot.

I offered to get a job to help out, but she had told me not yet, that my only goal was to get good grades so I could get into a good college and make something of myself.

Owen had worked in Corbin and had already gotten a job here at an ice cream parlor across town, but my mother wouldn't take the money he tried to give her. She was stubborn like that.

At that moment, as the smoke cloud no longer obscured my mother's face, I noticed the faint wrinkle lines near the corners of her mouth and on her forehead. These lines would become etchings over the next few weeks. Leaning against the porch railing, the smirk changed to a smile.

It was the last genuine smile I'd see from her for a long time.

"Hiya, neighbors!" a voice called from the sidewalk. I leaned to the left and looked, although I recognized the too-happy tone.

"Hello, Tim!" my mother said. She dropped her cigarette at her feet as casually as possible and squashed it with the toe of her non-slip work shoes. She was ashamed about her bad habit.

It didn't bother me. I liked the smell of fresh cigarette smoke. Now, whenever I chance upon that scent, it reminds me of her.

Tim Thompson was standing on our sidewalk with a small, old-school tape player clipped to his sweatpants. He wore over-the-ear headphones around his neck. In the stillness of the afternoon, an upbeat song floated toward the porch.

We got along well with Tim and Mary Thompson. They had been the previous new additions to the block, coming from Indiana a few months before us Carvers had arrived from Pennsylvania.

The Thompsons had taken us under their wings. Mr. Thompson was always looking for help with yard and house work. My first week in Pickwick, we laid a brick path in his backyard that went from his patio (everyone around here had patios, I swear) to his small shed.

I never got paid for my efforts—not in cash, at least—but Mrs. Thompson made a mean batch of chocolate chip cookies I was more than happy to take off her hands. The smell would drift through the open kitchen window, and my hunger pangs would kick into overdrive.

That was good motivation, let me tell you.

"How's it going?" Mr. Thompson asked. "You two enjoying this beautiful weather?"

He said *beautiful* like *bewwwtiful!* Very bubbly were the Thompsons.

"Oh, yes," my mother said. "It's a blessing in October." She cocked her head. "I didn't think you'd be back yet. How was...D.C., was it?"

"North Carolina, actually," Tim replied.

He clicked the pause button on the Walkman as he came up our driveway. At the porch steps, he stopped. A big and friendly smile was plastered across his face. He was a little sunburned on the bridge of his nose and on his brow.

His sweatpants were navy blue and they matched his sweatshirt, which had the N-D logo of the Fighting Irish printed across the chest. His brown hair was combed over in its usual way, partially obscuring the ever-growing bald spot atop his head.

Despite the smile and the patches of color on his skin, I thought he looked a little peaked, as if he'd just gotten off a long boat ride or hadn't slept well in a couple of days.

I didn't think much of it, though, knowing he had been on vacation for the last week. I knew firsthand how much traveling, even from southern Pennsylvania to Ohio, could wear you down.

"I thought you and Mary weren't due back until Monday," my mother said. "I was gonna send the boys over to rake your leaves before you got home."

I raised an eyebrow at the back of my mother's head. This was the first I was hearing of that plan. I should've expected it, though.

She was always trying to do these kind of kind things for the people in the neighborhood. I think because we were the only single-parent family on the block and she was worried about people talking behind our backs. She wanted to fit in despite us never being able to do so.

One thing I knew from a young age was that people were going to talk behind your back no matter what you did for them.

"That's mighty nice of you, Dolores," Mr. Thompson said. "But we had to cut the trip a couple days short. Mary had a bit of an accident."

My mother gasped. "Oh, no! Is she okay?"

Mr. Thompson waved his hand. "Yes, she's doing just fine. Nothing major. She just took a little tumble when we were out hiking. Stepped into a foxhole and turned her ankle pretty bad. It swelled up like a balloon, but the x-rays came back negative, thank the Holy Lord. Rest, ice, compress, and elevate is all they told us at the ER. Since we were pretty much there just to hike anyway, Mary wanted to come on back home. She'd rather recuperate in her own bed instead of her brother's guest room." Mr. Thompson glanced around and leaned closer as he whispered, "Between you and me, I wasn't really keen on sticking around there much longer. Her brother loves that Obama a little bit too much for my liking."

My mother chuckled uncomfortably. Politics were a sore spot with her.

"So you know how that is, I'm sure," Tim said.

"Well, I hope Mary is back on her feet soon! There's nothing worse than being stuck in bed when the weather's like this."

"You know," Mr. Thompson said, "I think she's enjoying the break. She'll be off work a few days longer, and that'll give her time to catch up on her soaps." He rolled his eyes and chuckled. "But don't get me started on those. That dang *Days of Our Lives* nonsense drives me batty."

My mother laughed with him, and then Mr. Thompson said, "All right, well, I'm gonna finish my workout here. It was great seeing you! I'm glad to be back in our wonderful neighborhood, that's for sure."

As he reached up to put his headphones over his ears, the right sleeve of his shifted down past his wrist and I caught a glimpse of a dingy white bandage near his forearm. Red so dark it was almost black had soaked through it.

I squirmed in my wicker chair, making it creak and groan.

"You okay, there, John?" Mr. Thompson asked.

"Yeah, sorry," I said. "I just saw..." I pointed to his arm. "I'm no good with blood, that's all."

"Ah, yes," Mr. Thompson replied, smoothing his sleeve down and rolling his eyes again. "Another vacation mishap, I'm afraid." He tittered—yes, *tittered*. "Although I enjoy my daily power walks, I am not much for hiking. It is more dangerous than I expected. Here on the sidewalks, I only have to worry about tripping on a crack or the occasional angry dog. It seems like everything is trying to get you out there in the wilderness."

"Well, I guess so," my mother said. "I believe I'll just stick to my books."

Mr. Thompson chortled. "Very good, Dolores! Ya can't get maimed by your imagination. That is very true."

"Give Mary our best. If you two need anything, the boys and I will be glad to help you out," my mother said.

Mr. Thompson smiled politely. "I will." We watched him go down the driveway before he stopped at the sidewalk, turned, and said, "You know I actually wouldn't mind a little help with the leaves. Being out of town and all has me a bit behind. And I'm not as young as I once was. They say your fifties are the new forties, but sometimes

I'll wake up with my joints so stiff I can barely get out of bed. And this gash I got on my arm makes dragging a rake through the lawn a bit more difficult. I'm sure I'll be fine in a week or so, but I don't want to be up to my neck in leaves by the time I'm ready to tackle the gutters." He snapped his fingers. "Speaking of the gutters, I'd love for Owen to lend me a hand with those. Athletic boy like himself, him and I will have them cleaned in no time."

My mother nodded. "I'll let Owen know soon as I see him. But I don't think John is doing anything tomorrow. Are you, John?"

Ugh.

"Nope," I said. "I'd be glad to help out."

Smiling, my mother leaned over and pinched my cheek like I was a baby. I hated when she did that.

"All right, I'll see you tomorrow, John! How's eight A.M. sound?"

It sounded terrible, but I flashed Mr. Thompson the O.K. symbol with my left hand.

"I don't know how much help I'll be," Mr. Thompson said, nodding toward his sleeve and the wound it was hiding, "but I won't be completely useless. Promise."

"Oh, please," my mother said. "You just worry about taking care of Mary. John'll be fine!"

"All right, well, I really appreciate it," Mr. Thompson said. "I'll get out of your hair now." He raised a hand and waved as he strolled past the front yard. We waved back.

I was grinning, and through my clenched teeth, I said in a low voice that Mr. Thompson couldn't hear, "Eight in the morning, really? It's the weekend!"

My mother waited until Mr. Thompson was past the tall hedges that separated our place from our next door neighbors before saying, "Waking up early is a good habit to have, love."

"I'll be glad to remind you of that next time you sleep in."

She hit me with a look that said *Try me, buddy*, and I blew her a kiss.

Somehow, and I don't understand it, my mother worked late almost every day of the week. Eight- to ten-hour shifts stuck on her feet, waiting on crowds of drunks, moving and grooving. But when she came home, she never crashed like a normal person would.

I'd hear her up and about, cleaning the house or doing laundry until three A.M., the TV on in the background. And even then, she never stayed asleep past eight.

I don't know how she did a lot of things, especially raising two boys on her own with little help, but she did it.

Like everything my mother did in life, she did it well.

"Go wake your brother," she said. "I'm gonna get dinner started, and I could use a hand from you two."

"Owen's not here," I said as I rolled my *Empire* magazine into a tube and rose from the wicker chair.

"When did he leave?"

I shrugged. "I haven't seen him since last night, right before he went and hung out with some friends."

My mother scratched her temple and squinted. "I could've sworn he was here when I left this morning."

I shook my head. "Not sure."

"So he never came home last night?" There was a note of alarm in her voice that I didn't like. "He was out all night?"

I shrugged again. "Maybe?"

But I was pretty sure he *had* been out all night.

My first thought was he was with a girl. They had spent the night together. Morning came around and he might've swung back home to brush his teeth and grab a fresh pair of Jockeys while my mother and I were asleep, and then it was right back to the girl's place.

That was the scenario in my head, at least. I didn't know if there was any truth to it, but *I* believed it.

I believed it because bad things—*truly* bad things—didn't happen in real life. Not mine. Those things were reserved for the movies.

But how wrong I was.

CHAPTER 2
THE SEARCH

I SENSED A RISING PANIC, but my mother went on like normal.

She gave Owen a call, said it had gone straight to voicemail. No big deal. That happened a lot because he had one of those flip phones you had to buy minutes for, and he was always texting his friends or girls, burning through the minutes.

"I just hope he's had a decent meal," my mother said, hanging the phone up on the wall by the kitchen doorway.

By this time, the chicken was already sizzling on the big skillet, filling the house with a smell that had my stomach growling.

"You boys are still growing. You need fuel!"

When the food was done, my mother and I sat

down at the table together and ate. It was delicious; no one could cook like my mother. But with Owen's spot empty, I started feeling a bit uneasy.

He was like most normal teenage boys in many ways, going out with his friends, sneaking beers when he could, girl-crazy,

What separated Owen from the others, I think, was how much he cared for his family —for us.

I couldn't remember a time he had ditched Saturday night dinner. Or any dinner, for that matter.

Saturdays and Sundays were big deals around the Carver house. Monday through Friday, my mother worked past midnight, so Owen and I had to fend for ourselves. When the weekend rolled around, she would go all out.

Sure, sometimes Owen had plans—what boy his age didn't?—but even if he did, he'd at the very least make an appearance. A no-show was completely out of character for him.

"Do you know who he was with last?" my mother asked me.

I was standing at the sink, the warm water washing away the suds on my plate. I turned the faucet off and scratched my forehead with a wet finger. The window was open, and the sun was on its way down.

"I think Ryan Kensington and Dave...something. I don't know his last name. But he's a big linebacker-looking kid."

"I know the Kensingtons. I'll give them a buzz. What do you think?"

I shrugged. When you're a teenager, there are fewer things more embarrassing than your mother calling to check up on you, but I knew Owen wouldn't mind. He never got embarrassed.

"Well, if he's not with Ryan, he's probably with some girl."

My mother frowned. "In that case, he *definitely* needs to come home."

Back then, phone books were still somewhat relevant (although they were on their way to being dubbed *Ancient)*. She found the Kensingtons' number at a speed that rivaled a Google search today.

Someone answered on the third ring. I heard a faint voice on the other end of the line.

"Hi, Dolores Carver here...yes...good, good, how about you? That's wonderful. I hate to call so late, but I'm looking for my son. His name is Owen." A pause. "Uh-huh...yes... Well, my youngest said he was out with your son last night—okay, can you ask him, please?"

Another pause while Mrs. Kensington fetched Ryan. Then the faint voice again. My mother tightened her grip on the phone and turned slightly away from me, as if she didn't want whatever was being said to reach my ears.

I stepped closer, straining to listen, catching snippets of words that I was able to work into full sentences. Something like: "Ryan says Owen went home last night around eleven. That was the last he heard from him."

Her voice raised and panicky, my mother said, "He didn't come home—" She flicked her eyes toward me and offered a reassuring smile. I was anything but reassured. "Okay, thank you," she continued. "If he comes around, please tell him to call his mother."

She hung up and stared at the phone for a long moment.

I stood a few feet away, waiting, unsure of what I should do. Unsure if I even could speak.

I cleared my throat and started to say I could try calling one of his other friends, but what other friends? I didn't know anyone. We hadn't been in town long.

It didn't matter; my mother was already dialing another number.

The Pickwick Police Department.

To tell you the truth, I was surprised she had opted to call the cops. She was always an optimist, a glass half-full type of person, and her going straight to the police after one call to the Kensington family seemed like it was her giving up hope.

In hindsight, I do agree with her actions, but as a teenager whose only brush with death up to that point had been the goldfish I won at the county fair when I was nine eating each other, it angered me.

My mother's conversation lasted about thirty seconds, and then a few minutes later a squad car pulled up our driveway.

A hefty cop asked us all the usual questions: could Owen have run away? Were there any problems at home? Could he have gone to our father's? What was he last wearing? Did we have a recent photo of him?

The officer scribbled down all of my mother's answers and then mine in a tiny notebook. He seemed uninterested, going through the motions.

He shook my mother's hand, then mine, and he said, "We'll get this info out on the wire ASAP. But Miss Carver, don't worry. Your son's a big boy. He'll show up."

"What should I do?" my mother asked. There were tears in her eyes. It was odd.

"Sit tight and wait. He'll turn up. No sense going to look for him in the dark, especially when the moon is pretty much full tonight." He chuckled. "You know what they say about the full moon, huh? That's when all the freaks come out."

We didn't laugh, and a shimmer of regret passed over the cop's face, but he wasn't about to admit any wrongdoing.

He grumbled, hitched up his belt, and patted me on the back as he left. "Take care of your mother, all right, young man?"

I said nothing, but closed the door as soon as he set foot on the porch and went to where my mother was sitting on the couch, her face buried in her hands.

"Owen's okay, Mom. He's a smart kid. I bet he'll come walking through the door any minute now."

She sprang up and beelined to her purse on the

dining room table. Her keys jingled as she yanked them out.

"'*Sit tight and wait,*' my ass," she mumbled to herself before turning to me and saying, "I want you to stay here in case he comes back. Understood?"

"Mom—"

But she was gone before I could stand.

I usually listened to my mother, but I didn't that night.

As soon as she backed down the driveway, I got my rusty Schwinn out of the garage and went riding around the block, calling my brother's name.

After about an hour of this, I realized how each time his name left my mouth, my voice felt weaker. I also didn't know the layout of the town much, and I was pretty sure I was going to get lost if I kept on going.

With the swollen moon above and the cop's words about all the freaks coming out echoing in my head, I'll admit I was more than a little scared.

The town felt eerily desolate for a Saturday night. Besides the same pizza delivery car making the rounds, I'd seen no other cars or people. Most houses were dark and lifeless.

Then something weird happened near the old rundown factories.

I stopped and checked before I crossed the intersection. When I looked in front of me, I saw a dog sitting on the opposite sidewalk by a bench.

I would've noticed it had it been there a second ago. Beyond the bench was an empty field that led to the dark (and very creepy) woods. The pool of light cast by the streetlights reached a hundred or so feet into the overgrown grass. If the dog had been crossing the field, I would've seen and probably heard it coming, right?

Weirder still, the dog wasn't just looking at me. It was looking *into* me.

I squinted, trying to identify the breed or whether or not I'd seen it around town before. I was pretty sure I hadn't because I would've definitely remembered.

This dog was…unique. I thought it looked like a Dalmatian, at least from its face, ears, and the way it sat, but instead of white fur with black spots, it was the other way around: mostly black fur with white spots.

An inverted Dalmatian.

Dangling from its pale blue collar was a tag. I scanned the area for its owner.

Some people were confident enough in their training to let their dog walk around without a leash as they went along a few paces behind them, but there was no one else in sight.

The dog had to have been lost. If I could see from where, maybe I could return it to its owner, or at least keep it until I could—although I wasn't sure how my mother would've felt about that.

Still, it was better than turning the other way and letting the poor thing starve or get hit by a car.

Slow and easy so I wouldn't startle it, I climbed off of my bike and guided it across the street.

The dog cocked its head, still staring at me. When I was about halfway across, it stood on all fours.

I stopped, thinking it was about to bolt. It didn't, but it walked back and forth a few times in front of the bench.

Its footsteps were silent. No nails clicking on the concrete, collar not jingling.

I stuck out my left hand, fingers curled downward in a show of truce.

"Hey puppy, whatcha doing out here all alone?" I smacked my lips together to make a kissing noise.

"It's okay, buddy. Let me help get you back home. I bet your owner is worried sick about you—"

"Mind your business, pal," spoke a low, echoing voice.

"What?" I squinted again and looked around. The sound had come from in front of me, but I saw nobody past the bench. "Who said that? Hey, is this your dog?"

Something howled in the distance.

Chills rolled down my back. What the hell was that? A wolf? But what was wrong with it? It sounded...*insane.*

The dog's ears perked up, its eyes widened, and it focused its eyes in the direction of the howling. Then it spun around and took off toward the factory building.

"Hey, wait—!"

I dropped my bike and ran a few steps after it, but it moved lightning-quick and was soon gone to the shadows.

I considered a chase.

At least I did until I looked at the buildings. Broken windows stared back at me like the eyes of the dead.

These were the corpses of Pickwick's urban industrialization, and the idea of coming across what *things* might await inside had me back on my bike, standing on the pedals and working my legs into overdrive.

I didn't slow until I hit Whitehall Road and saw my house sitting on the corner.

Despite my frantic prayers, Owen was not home. Neither was my mother. I locked the deadbolt and turned on a channel that was playing old *Looney Tunes* reruns.

My mother got back sometime after one A.M. I knew this because I was still awake on the couch (I wouldn't have been able to sleep even if I tried).

And she came back alone.

A couple more days passed without any sign of Owen's whereabouts. It was Tuesday. I don't think I had slept more than a handful of hours since Saturday. I also didn't go to school and no one seemed to mind that.

Ryan and Dave had already talked to the cops, but the story they fed them was a much-neutered version of what eventually would be revealed to have happened.

I believe Ryan was the orchestrator of that, too

afraid they'd question him about the booze and how drunk they'd gotten, where they'd gotten it, and his dad would kick his ass.

In their initial story, they'd only been cruising around and listening to music for an hour or two when Owen grew upset about something Dave said. He was apparently so mad, he decided to walk home.

Let me tell you, that didn't sound a thing like my brother. He never got *that* pissed. Neither Ryan or Dave had seen or heard from him since.

On that Tuesday night, Dave called my house and he told my mother the truth.

I listened to the conversation from the corded phone in the kitchen. If my mother knew about this, she didn't stop me.

Dave said they were out drinking by the old abandoned factories. Yes, the same factories I had seen that dog.

They dared Owen to head into the woods and call the Hollow Witch, some local urban legend that was basically a rip-off of Bloody Mary. Owen took on the dare.

He was in there for maybe five minutes before they heard him scream.

"There was a sound," Dave told my mother.

"Like a growl from, I dunno, a bear or something, and then Owen started yelling like crazy."

"A bear?" my mother repeated. "Are you sure?"

"No...I dunno. It was weird, that's all. Like some kind of cross between a person screaming and an animal howling."

"Okay, young man, did you tell the police this?"

"No. They wouldn't have believed me. And Ryan was scared about them finding out we were drinking—"

My mother hung up. I did the same in the kitchen quickly after.

She dialed the police department's number. I didn't bother listening to this conversation.

My mind was busy remembering the howling I had heard on Saturday night. Hadn't it been...*off?* Could it have been from the same animal Dave described?

My stomach felt like it was full of lead.

What the hell happened to my brother?

So, even though Dave's story didn't fully check out and Ryan contradicted some of it, we now had a place to search.

The next morning, my mother, a couple dozen volunteers, a few police officers, and myself set out among the woods where the Hollow Witch was rumored to stalk.

We combed through the area for an hour before someone called out that they had found something. It was Mr. Thompson.

My mother and I rushed to where he was at, about fifty or so feet away from a large, defaced boulder known as Blood Rock.

My mind was spinning as I followed my mother through the tangles of decrepit vines and branches, thinking I was about to see my older brother's dead body.

Mr. Thompson was holding up a stick. Hanging from it by the laces was a well-worn black and white Converse All Star sneaker.

My mother gasped and stumbled. Someone steadied her before helping her sit on a smaller rock nearby.

As I looked at the shoe, I didn't gasp or scream, but I felt something deflate deep inside of me... because there was blood on it.

It wasn't long before they found his body.

My mother and I were not there when it happened. I am glad for that. Seeing it might've killed her, and it might've killed me too.

At the very least, I know I would've never been able to shake the image from my mind.

What I thought of Owen Christopher Carver—all those good memories, the fun times, the laughs, the pranks, even the scuffles that are unavoidable amongst two brothers close in age—would've been buried by what I saw.

I have since read the reports, gone over the descriptions—sparse yet effective—but I made sure my copies came without photographs. All these years later, I'm still not ready to see what had happened to my brother.

It pains me to even think about it.

And rather than ruin your day, all I'll say is that something had ripped Owen apart. It had tore him open, shredded his flesh. He was found with a broken neck and missing many of his vital organs.

The latter was a detail that swept through town, and the students at Pickwick High took it and ran with it.

The Hollow Witch was back, and she was hungry for the hearts of the young! I did my best to ignore it, but it was hard. The whispers, the pointing behind my back I never saw but could feel, all of that chipped away at me.

Owen's death was officially ruled an accident *"caused by undetermined factors."*

In the coroner's report, the animal predation had been listed as post-mortem. They found no human DNA on the body. No signs of foul play.

The theory was this: Owen, a little too drunk, had taken a bad fall in the woods and broken his neck. Then, coyotes or a pack of starving stray dogs (was the one I'd seen by the abandoned factories part of this pack?) decided to dine on my freshly deceased brother.

Mystery solved. Investigation over. Right?

No.

I knew it was bullshit.

And I was going to find out the truth.

CHAPTER 3
A GIFT

I NEVER REALLY KNEW WHAT I wanted to do when I grew up. Most kids, they want to be professional athletes or doctors or veterinarians, but none of those occupations intrigued me.

My mother would often suggest I become a teacher or an engineer, get a steady job…only I hated school, and I wasn't bright enough to be an engineer.

I remember being bummed out after a career day activity we had during my freshman year of high school. People from various "respected" job fields spoke at an assembly about what they did, and then the students had to take a test to help turn us in the right direction.

I somehow got *logger* as my most compatible

career, but I had never lifted an axe in my life, I was a weakling, and I hated splinters.

My classmates scored jobs like *electrician* and *manager* and *fashion designer* and financial advisor. I think one boy even got *race car driver*.

And here I was getting called "Paul Bunyan" by the ruder kids. That didn't really bother me. They'd called me worse things back in Pennsylvania.

What did bother me was the existential crisis that the career day had thrown me in. What the hell was I going to do when I got older? How was I going to survive?

So when I got home later that day, I did what I always did when I was upset. I plopped down on the couch and popped my old VHS copy of *The Empire Strikes Back* into the tape player.

Owen came through the front door around the time Luke Skywalker was training with Yoda on Dagobah. He sat next to me, but he didn't watch the movie.

"Something wrong?" he asked.

I shook my head.

"Don't lie, Johnny."

"I'm not."

"I may seem like it sometimes, but I'm not

stupid," Owen said. "*Empire* is basically your *Mystic Pizza.*"

That was a reference to the movie my mother always turned on when she was down in the dumps.

I sighed.

There was no point lying to Owen—he saw through everything. I told him about the career day and how I was destined to be Paul Bunyan while my peers got to design dresses for supermodels and race cars at tracks around the world at three hundred miles per hour.

Owen listened without saying a word. He was good at that, listening. When I was finished, he cracked a smile.

"Yeah, it's dumb, I know," I said. "I just want to be happy."

"No, man. It's not dumb. We're all trying to figure it out. Life, I mean. Go ahead and walk into any *respectable* place of employment and tell me those people got it figured out. You can't because they don't. No one really does. If they did, if someone had all the answers, they woulda wrote a book about it already."

"Yeah?"

"Definitely." Owen turned toward the television. It was an old Zenith with a number pad in the front and an aluminum-colored case, its screen not large or clear enough to do any *Star Wars* film justice.

Luke Skywalker had just decapitated the apparition of Darth Vader with his lightsaber. The black helmet rolled to his feet, and the mask exploded open, revealing the face inside to be—*gasp!*—Luke's own.

"Whatever you end up doing," Owen said, "you'll be great at it." He grunted as he got off the couch and patted me on the shoulder. "Hell, you could be the next George Lucas or Spielberg if you wanted to, Johnny. But you'll never know unless you go for it."

And that was when it clicked. It was so obvious, staring me right in the face, that I felt like an idiot for not realizing.

They say the magic goes, but it doesn't have to. Because there's one place the magic exists forever, and that place is on the silver screen.

In the movies, action heroes were riddled with bullets and still got up to walk away from a huge explosion. Monsters and aliens and giant sharks with vendettas and whatever else you could imagine terrorized the characters and audiences alike.

In the movies, the good guys won and the bad

guys lost. I loved that more than anything else. I didn't care if I got paid or if I got famous or if my films sucked.

I didn't care about any of that at all.

The only thing I did care about was having fun.

But, as I'm sure you know, life doesn't always happen the way you think it will.

Sometimes…the monsters are real.

Owen's death about killed my mother.

We buried him on a Saturday morning, in the Pickwick cemetery near my grandmother and grandfather, both lifelong residents of the town.

There is a lot I choose to block out about that time, and there is a lot I have buried deep in my subconscious, but from what I remember, for a kid who had just moved to Pickwick only a few months before his passing, Owen's memorial service was nice.

Well, as nice as a funeral can be, I guess.

Nearly all the town turned out to pay their respects. Even Mayor Tyson showed up. I shook a lot of hands, hugged nearly every woman over the age of sixty (I swear all of them wore the same flowery perfume), and developed sore spots on both my shoulder blades from the overly macho men patting their condolences and telling me it was going to be okay and how Owen was in a better place now and *blah-blah-blah.*

I disagreed. He had just been eighteen years old at the time of his death. His future was a blank slate. He could've been anything he wanted to be, done anything he wanted to do, and now he was gone.

Funerals and memorial services are things supposed to help the living with moving on, right? You grieve for a period of time, you accept that your loved one isn't coming back, and then you get better. What doesn't kill you makes you stronger and all that.

I thought that was crap.

Neither my mother or myself moved on after the services. It was difficult when reminders of Owen were all over the place.

His winter boots by the door, never to be laced up again; his bedroom with its posters of LeBron James and Led Zeppelin and a sultry Katy Perry on the walls, the door cracked open, it insides peeking at us like red meat through a slit in the skin; old pieces of art he made as a kid on the refrigerator;

trophies on the mantel (being the athlete he was, he had a lot of those).

But then one evening, I don't know, maybe two months after Owen died, my mother and I were watching some old black and white gangster movie on the couch—an edited television version with sadly almost no blood or cursing—and my mother asked for the remote.

I grabbed it off the coffee table and handed it to her. I thought she was going to change the channel but she didn't. She just stared at it for an alarmingly long time. Was she having a stroke or something?

I cleared my throat. "Mom? You okay?"

"Yeah, I'm okay. I'm just…just thinking."

"About what?"

She shrugged, her eyes shiny with tears. "Owen." She smiled. "I miss him, and I hope he's okay."

"He is, Mom. He is."

After that, things slowly started getting better.

It was December 2008 and I had been shoveling our driveway early that morning so my mother could get the car out of the garage and make it to work on time. I was already booked through the whole afternoon thanks to her calling around the neighborhood and offering my shoveling services.

We were a week out from Christmas and Pickwick High was on holiday break, and there wasn't much else to do. The shoveling was hard, but it kept my mind busy and my head strangely empty.

The snow had come down in droves the night before. Not the light and fluffy flakes you see in movies, but wet, heavy stuff perfect for making snowmen and snowballs and throwing a wrench in your travel plans. Shoveling it did a number on my lower back and arms, but I was young, I'd be okay.

The temperature outside was in the twenties, and the wind had a sharp bite we rarely felt in Pennsylvania.

I bundled up in my heavy winter coat, a knit hat, gloves, and a pair of snow pants. By the time I was done, I had taken my hat off to find that my hair was stuck to my forehead in sweaty strands.

I was beyond exhausted, but hey, at least my mother could get to work. And being on break, I could go back to sleep.

I set my boots out to dry by the register in our tiny foyer and hung my coat up over the railing of the stairs, then I went into the kitchen for a glass of water.

My mother was waiting for me with a goofy grin on her face and her hands behind her back.

I stopped, brushed my hair out of my eyes. "Why are you being weird, Mom?"

I half-expected her to be holding a pamphlet for a Bible school or tickets to this ultra-religious Christmas play she had mentioned attending a few days earlier.

"I'm sorry, John. I'm too dang excited."

"Excited for what?"

She squealed. "I was going to wait until Christmas but I can't anymore. And with you being on break and all, I thought now's a perfect time to put it to use."

"Put *what* to use?"

She shrugged.

"Is it a new shovel?"

My mother shook her head and stepped closer. I looked at her suspiciously. This was out of character, all the giddiness. "Close your eyes."

"What? Mom, seriously?"

"Don't give me that snark now, John." With a huff, she blew a strand of her blonde hair out of her face. "Just humor me for a second here, please." That was more like her. "I know you're all big and grown up now," she continued, "but you're always gonna be my baby whether you like it or not."

I sighed and closed my eyes.

"Okay…now hold out your hands."

I did. She placed a small-ish box in them. It was slick with wrapping paper, and atop it was a frilly bow. It weighed a few pounds.

Whatever was inside was solid. I had no idea what it could've been. A new Bible? A brick? So I did the thing you're supposed to do when you get a present. I shook the box, and my mother immediately squealed in horror, as if there was actually a puppy inside.

"No! Don't shake it!"

"Sorry."

"Jonathan Dell Carver, if you broke it I am going to kick your behind."

"Well…then, what is it?"

"Open it and find out."

I slid into a chair at the kitchen table and scooted away a stack of bills lodged beneath the placemat. I set the box in front of me.

My mother watched with an anticipation and excitement in her eyes I don't believe I've ever seen.

She laced her fingers together and held them up against her chin. "Go on…"

First, I slowly undid the bow, racking my brain for what my mother could be this excited over, and then I unpeeled a corner of the wrapping paper, tearing down a long sliver.

A large "C" showed through. I recognized that "C," and my stomach twisted. I let out a soft gasp and whispered, "Holy shit."

"Hey! Language, John!"

"Sorry, Mom. But…you didn't…no fuh—*fricking* way."

My mother nodded. "I know you've been wanting one. Owen told me, and I think that's a great idea. You are so talented, honey. So creative!"

I stared at the "C" on the box and felt like I was dreaming. It wasn't long after that reality came crashing down. I resisted ripping anymore wrapping paper off and pushed the box away. I couldn't keep this gift. We couldn't afford it.

"John? What's wrong?"

"Mom…I can't. This is too much."

"You're being silly."

I sighed and looked at her. "You can't afford this…"

"Nonsense! It was on sale!" She looked down at the tiled floor. "I wish I could get you a car—"

"Mom, to me, this is better than a car."

"It's last year's model, and it's refurbished," she said. "Which is how I got it at such a good price. But the man at Best Buy said it was still one of the best on the market. Heck of a deal."

"It still had to be like a million bucks."

My mother set a finger on her lips, which were raised in a smile, and she shook her head. "I'll never tell. Just finish opening it, okay? I want to see."

I stared at the box for a long time.

My mother came around and leaned on my shoulder. "Really," she said in a serious tone, "it wasn't that much. And you deserve it, John. You help me out more than you know. You're a great kid. I am *so* proud of you."

She kissed the top of my head. Her voice was getting weepy. I'll admit, I felt tears burning in my eyes too.

"Thank you, Mom."

"It's an investment, John. When you're a hot-shot director like Steven Spielberg, you can buy me a mansion and a Corvette, and we'll call it square."

I laughed. "Spielberg? I think that's setting the bar a little too high."

"Too high? Nothing's too high for my boy! You'll be better than Spielberg and Kubrick and all of them combined, I know it! But you won't be better than anyone…if you don't accept the dang gift already!" She nodded at the box.

I gave in. I couldn't help it. I tore off the wrapping paper and dug into the box.

From it, I pulled out a refurbished Canon Vixia YX20 HD camcorder. Aside from a few scratches on the casing there was no way you could tell it was used. The lens and the LCD screen were untouched.

I powered it on. The battery indicator flashed red, but I had enough time to check all the buttons and play with the zoom slider.

It all worked, and the picture on the viewfinder was sharp as ever. With a huge grin on my face, I pointed the lens at my mother.

"Nuh-uh, no you don't." She jumped away into the hall and half-hid herself behind the door frame. "If I'm gaining an extra ten pounds, I wanna at least earn it by scarfing down a bunch of jelly donuts."

The battery indicator flashed another warning on the screen, telling me the camera was about to die. I shut it down, unfurled the charging cable, and plugged it in on the counter next to the blender.

Safe from being recorded, my mother stepped back into the kitchen. "You like it, then?"

I didn't know what to say for a while. I just stood there in the kitchen and looked at her. My head was filled with a million words I *wanted* to say, but all the excitement mixed them into a big melting pot of nonsense.

Finally, I said, "Mom, I love it. Thank you so, so much." I bolted over to her, and I hugged her so hard she wheezed.

"Good, good." She kissed me on the cheek. "Now, what's the first John Carver picture going to be about?"

"Picture? You're really dating yourself there, Ma."

"Hey now, watch it, buster. You know what I meant."

I shrugged. "Hm…I've got no idea. That's a lot of pressure there, my first *picture*."

Like the words of gratitude and appreciation for my mother had been jumbled in my head, so were all my story ideas. The seeds had been planted a long time ago, but none of the crops had fully bloomed yet—I think because I never truly thought

I'd be able to do it. It always seemed like a pipe dream. With the camera, it didn't seem so far-fetched now.

"I want to do a sci-fi epic," I said, "like *Star Wars*, but I don't have the budget for that. It'd probably just come off looking silly."

"So what?" My mother's face turned serious. "There's nothing wrong with looking silly as long as what you create is heartfelt and *real*. You just have to put a piece of yourself into it. That's art, right?"

My eyes widened. "Wow, Mom, that's really…deep."

"Eh, I heard something like it in one of my community college classes. Funny, it's one of the few things during those three semesters that actually stuck. My poetry instructor said it, Mrs. Burns."

I made an explosion sound. "*What?* You went to college? *And* you write poetry?"

"*Wrote*. I haven't picked up the pen in a *loooong* time. It was only a few semesters, then I got pregnant with…" She trailed off, her eyes drifting toward a picture of Owen on the refrigerator. He was seven or eight in the picture, dressed in his soccer uniform, holding a ball and flashing a smile with a missing front tooth. "Well, you know. Life and all that."

"You can always go back."

She nodded, a touch of sadness in her eyes I didn't like seeing but was growing used to.

"Maybe one day. If God wills it." She looked at the clock. "I'm glad you like your gift, honey, but I've gotta run. You keep thinking about that first *picture* of yours. I want to be the first one to see it." She pinched me on the cheek.

She left, and I sat down in the living room with the camera's box in my hand.

On the back was a collection of crystal-clear images: people on the beach caught mid-stride with big smiles on their faces, a toddler blowing out her birthday candles, a dog darting through a backyard with a stick clamped between its jaws.

Beautiful snapshots that made me want to rush outside and start shooting my own footage. Maybe it would one day end up on a Canon box.

Problem was, the battery needed charging...and I had to go shovel those last few driveways.

The thought of skimping out on the work was pretty enticing, I'll tell you that. I knew if I did, though, I'd never hear the end of it from my mother.

After a few minutes, I threw on a fresh set of

warm clothes, hopped in my damp boots and shrugged into my winter coat.

The snow had stopped, but the wind had picked up, howling like a rabid wolf, shrill and crazy.

I'll tell you I almost turned around and went back inside as soon as I felt that bitter air hit my face.

I'm glad I didn't, though.

If I had, I would've never met the kid who would become my best friend. And without him, I don't think I would be here telling you this story.

We stared down the face of evil together, and because we had each other's backs, we lived to tell the tale.

CHAPTER 4
THE OTHER NEW KID

HAVE you ever shoveled wet snow for hours on end? If you have, you know it sucks, plain and simple. It sucks pretty bad.

Five *long* driveways later, I was ready to call it quits. My mother wouldn't be home until around seven, so I figured I'd grab a quick bite to eat, wash up, and then start dinner for her as a thank you for the early Christmas gift. Something simple, like grilled cheese and some tomato soup. I wasn't much of a cook, but I'd spice the dish up with oyster crackers.

I walked down the street, my boots struggling for traction in the slush. The sidewalks were mostly buried by the snow.

Roads weren't much better, honestly, but there

were barely any cars to watch out for. The smarter folks would be huddled up inside their homes, safe and warm.

I turned off Dart and onto Parkway Extension to walk the short curve toward Whitehall, where my place sat on the corner.

For a while, I had heard nothing but the wind blowing in short gusts, threatening to take my hat with it, but as I rounded the curve, I heard the familiar sound of a plastic scraping against concrete.

On my right a short boy hacked away at the snow near the end of his drive with a shovel. I didn't recognize him from school or from around the neighborhood.

We caught eyes, and I waved.

The boy didn't wave back, but he stared nervously a moment and then snapped his eyes down to the task at hand, grunting as he threw a shovelful of snow over his shoulder.

The wind snatched it and blew a white cloud onto the drive, dusting the back of his red-and-black checkered coat. This was not a winter coat, I should add. Nor was his hat built for these temperatures.

The coat would barely keep you warm during

the fall, and the hat I wasn't sure about. It wasn't one I'd seen before. It was shaped like a basket and had an Oriental rug-type pattern of beads on it.

Also, I was pretty sure he was wearing a dress beneath everything.

Now, don't get me wrong, I have nothing against males wearing dresses—whatever makes you happy. But to fifteen-almost-sixteen-year-old me, who had not seen more than a few square miles of Pennsylvania and Ohio, the idea was kind of crazy. Especially when it was below freezing out.

The boy sensed me staring again, because he turned and stared back for a moment.

I got a real good look at him this time. He wasn't white, like ninety-eight percent of the residents of Pickwick, but he wasn't Black either. His skin was more of a tan color—Indian or Middle Eastern. Despite the bit of facial hair on his face, I reckoned he was around my age.

And again, I waved, opening my mouth to say something. I don't know what.

"*Hello!*" or maybe "*I'm John. Who might you be, pal?*" because the Pickwick friendliness had started to rub off on me, but the boy dropped his shovel and power-walked toward his garage.

Only…he slipped on a patch of ice, and his tennis shoes gave out on him.

The shovel flew from his hands in an almost exaggerated, comical way, and he pinwheeled his arms for balance. His act of falling couldn't have lasted more than a few seconds, but when I replay it in my head now, the boy seemed like he was sliding and flapping his arms all over the driveway before he finally thumped in a pile of snow by the garage.

I ditched my shovel and went carefully toward him, but apparently I hadn't gone carefully enough, and I must've hit the same patch of ice he had. I slid like Tom Cruise in that famous scene from *Risky Business* right into the garage door, and then took a hard seat in the snow.

Dazed, I lay there looking up at the darkening sky. What was left of the sun (not much) was blacked out by the backlit figure of the boy.

"Are you okay?" he said in an accent that I couldn't pinpoint, as if he was trying to blend his home country's manner of speaking with the suburban Ohio way.

He offered me a hand and helped me to my feet. Although I hadn't yet had my last and best growth spurt, I towered over him.

"Yeah, think so." I dusted snow from my pants.

It was already melting and soaking through the material. "You?"

"It could have been worse, I suppose," said the boy.

"I'm John."

The boy hunched his shoulders and spoke in a whisper. "I am Ali Bu Ali Al-Kareem."

I blinked at him, trying to wrap my mind around what he said. After a moment, I managed, "Wow, that's a lot of names."

"Just Ali is fine."

I laughed. "All right, Just Ali."

Ali cocked his head. "Pardon?"

"It's a joke," I said. "Never mind. So…you moved here not long ago, yeah?"

The house had been up for sale around the time my family and I left Pennsylvania. Sometime in September, the FOR SALE sign was replaced with a SALE PENDING sign that hung around for as long as I could remember.

He nodded. "Yes. My father, my older brother, and myself moved here from the Middle East three weeks ago." He winced as he said this, and I didn't understand why for a while.

Remember, this was 2008-going-on-2009, not even a decade after the tragedy of 9/11. At the mention of the Middle East or Islam or Arabs, back then—and even to this day—the first thought that comes to a lot of Americans' minds is *terrorism*. When Ali told me where he was from, I just thought it was—

"Cool," I said, and Ali relaxed. "You wanna know how I could tell you weren't from around here? And no, it's not your accent."

Again, the expectant and slightly disappointed expression seized his features.

"Because you're dressed like you've never seen snow before," I said.

"Ah." Ali nodded. "That is because I have never seen it before. There is not much of anything besides hot weather in Oman."

I recognized the name of the country, but Ali had pronounced it as *Oh-mon*. Stupid me always thought it was pronounced like it was spelled: *Oh-man*.

"In Oman," Ali continued, "there is only summer and hotter summer. Snow has always seemed like a fable to my family and I."

"A fable?"

"Yes, because we have only seen such an occurrence at the cinema."

"Wow." I adjusted my hat, shifting away the

sweaty locks of hair that clung to my forehead. "I always thought *everyone* saw snow at some point. That's crazy."

"We barely see rain."

"Shit," I said. "Earth is a large place, I guess. My worldview's already expanding."

"That is a good thing. I, too, have expanded my mind in my three short weeks here."

"Good, good," I said. Dreading the awkward silence that was sure to follow, I added, "Well, you want some help?"

"Help?"

I pointed to the driveway. "Shoveling this crap. I've been at it all day. Shoveled the Thompson place down there, the Maleri place, and Old Man Gunthrie's. I'm basically a pro shoveler at this point."

"*You* would help *me?*" Ali sounded astonished.

I shrugged. "Why not? One more won't hurt. And this driveway ain't got shit on the Maleris'."

"It is just…" He shook his head. "Never mind. I suppose if you do not mind, I would be quite grateful to, uh, receive it. If my abi—my *father*—sees I have yet to finish this task, I am afraid he will be sorely disappointed."

I clapped Ali on the back. He felt very thin and bony beneath his clothes. "Then let's get to it."

We did, tearing through that snow like human snowplows. While we worked, I tried to get to know Ali better. He seemed like a good guy, a genuine guy, but I could tell he was afraid of something and I wanted to help him...I don't know, not feel so afraid.

"So you're from Oman? I've heard of it, but I couldn't point it out on a map."

"It is not well known in America, that is true. Do you know where Saudi Arabia is?"

"Yeah, I think so."

"Oman shares a border with Saudi Arabia, as well as Yemen and the U.A.E."

"U.A.E.?"

"United Arab Emirates," Ali said.

I stopped shoveling, stood up, and scratched my forehead beneath my damp hat. "Man, I really need to brush up on my geography. It's always been my worst *Jeopardy!* category."

Ali smiled. "I love that show!"

"Who doesn't? It's a treasure." I grinned. "Why'd you come here of all places? To Ohio? I mean, it's basically the junkyard of America."

"I was led to believe Florida possessed that title," Ali said.

"Yeah, well, I guess maybe America has two junkyards."

"That is most unfortunate."

I stared at him, expecting a smile or something to indicate he was joking, but his face was all business. I couldn't help myself. I burst out laughing.

"What is it that you find so humorous?" Ali asked.

Once I got control of myself, I said, "I dunno, man. Just how you're, like, serious all the time, even when we're talking about junkyards."

Ali was always thinking people were making fun of him in America. For the most part, he was right.

I saw it firsthand in school. Kids, especially teenagers, are jerks. Although I was a teenager myself—and maybe a little bit of an asshole sometimes too—I never made fun of Ali.

There wasn't anything to make fun of. He might've been a little short, but why would I care about that? It would be nice to have someone I could actually beat in basketball to play with.

Really, I could find nothing wrong about the guy. He was smart as all hell, handsome (Ohio girls seemed to dig that exotic caramel-colored skin of his), and funny in his own innocent sort of way.

To most everyone else, I guess they were blind to his positive attributes. All they saw was his skin color—how he was not *white*. Maybe they felt threatened by that or uncomfortable, I don't know.

But I do know that life is all about being uncomfortable.

You think the first time you saw the cold light in the delivery room, you were comfortable? Or how about when you took your first step?

Nope.

You were content in a sac of fluid in your mother's uterus. And then you were content with staying low to the floor, crawling.

That's kind of how it was with Ali. If I had just brushed him off as the new kid who was a different color than me, who worshiped a different god, who spoke a little oddly, then I would've missed out on so much.

"John, do forgive me for saying so, but you are…different," Ali said as we threw shovelfuls of snow behind us.

We had almost finished our respective halves of the driveway, both of us now almost ass-to-ass in the middle, when a silver Mercedes pulled in, its tires crunching loose chunks of snow that had escaped the piles.

I gawked at the car. I had never seen one like it.

"Oh no, he is early," Ali muttered.

I thought I saw a flash of terror in his eyes.

Not really thinking much about it, I looked away from him and back at the car. The Mercedes was old but in great shape. It was like something you'd see Sean Connery's version of James Bond driving off into the sunset in, a blonde bombshell leaning on him from the passenger's seat and a confident look of satisfaction on Bond's face.

The engine turned off, the headlights winked out, and the door opened soundlessly. Out of the car stepped a man of about sixty or so.

His hair and beard were both gray, and he wore thick-lensed glasses at the end of his nose and the same type of hat Ali wore on his head. But he had the good sense to wear a thick winter coat.

Ali stood ramrod straight, coming to attention like a soldier in the military. The smile and carefree expression that was on his face a moment ago vanished.

Ali's father slammed the car door hard enough for its echo to travel all throughout the still neighborhood. I looked him in the eyes, and his nostrils flared, but he smiled in this polite way that rubbed me wrong. His face was hard, weathered, and I sensed anger boiling beneath his forced-friendly exterior.

"Hello," I said. "I'm John. I was just helping Ali here clear the driveway. These winters are back-breaking—"

"Thank you. Nice to have met you, John, but Ali must be coming inside for...dinner now."

He nodded at me and then turned to Ali. He said something in Arabic. Ali replied softly at first, but his father said something that Ali didn't like and the conversation grew more animated, his hands moving, his head bobbing, both giving me sidelong glances every now and again.

I stood there twirling my shovel in the snow. I wished I knew what they were saying. Nowadays, I know I'm probably better off not knowing.

Sensing a more heated discussion, I cleared my throat. Neither of them noticed.

"All right, yeah, it was nice meeting you, Ali. I hope we can hang out again before the break's over. If not, I guess I'll see you at school."

Ali smiled. "It was very nice to meet you as well, John. I, too, hope—"

His father snapped at him in Arabic.

"Goodbye, John," Ali said.

I waved to them and headed home.

The whole time I was trudging through the snow, I was thinking I might've made a new friend.

That was a weird thing to think about. Friends had never been my specialty. I got along pretty well with people when I had to, but I was no stranger to closing myself off, sometimes accidentally, an attribute of mine that got even worse after Owen died.

With Ali, I don't know what it was, but I had this feeling about him. Hell, he could've been a *best* friend.

I was right about that, but this wouldn't happen for a few more weeks. See, Ali's father, in his quest to remain as inconspicuous to the people of Pickwick as possible, decided to continue Ali's studies at home.

Homeschooling wasn't an uncommon thing back then—not as common as it is today—but Ali's father worked a lot and his mother was back in Oman, which meant Ali was left on his own for the majority of the day.

A curious boy will be a curious boy, strict father or not, I believe. So, although Ali wanted to obey his father and not bring attention to himself or the rest of the family, he let that curiosity win out one boring afternoon and he left the house to explore the town. On Center Street, his eyes were caught by a model train in the display window of a small antique shop.

If it had been any other business, Ali might've been in the clear. Unfortunately, Grover's Collectibles was run by an old Vietnam War veteran, who wasn't exactly welcoming to foreigners and had increasingly grown more hostile against Arabic people, no matter their country or origin, after 9/11.

Around one on a Wednesday in February, 2009, Ali entered the shop. The place was always dead except for maybe on the weekend of the Harvest Festival, where nearly every out-of-towner within a fifteen-mile radius decided to hang around Pickwick's downtown area on Center Street. The bell above the door rang, and Bill Grover's eyes automatically went to the entrance as he put on a practiced salesman's smile. When he saw his newest potential customer wasn't white, the smile turned to a scowl. He snapped his newspaper shut, tore off his reading glasses, and immediately went on the offensive.

"Help ya?" he asked curtly.

"Hello, sir," Ali replied. "No, thank you. I am only browsing."

Bill Grover nodded, folding his thick, hairy arms over a chest that was a bit more flabby than it had been back in 'Nam.

Ali told me he was only in the place for a few minutes, but Bill Grover stuck to him like a shadow. He didn't even try to be coy about it. He dragged his foot a little harder to make himself known and grumbled and grunted if Ali got too close to some of his overpriced junk. Ali was particularly fond of a model train visible through the show window, and when he leaned over the platform it sat on to check the price—Ali had saved a decent amount of money over the last year in preparation for his trek to the United States—Bill Grover's curtness turned to outright rudeness.

"What's a kid like you doing here now? Ain't you supposed to be in school?"

"I am homeschooled, sir," Ali answered. "I wish to attend the local high school, but my family and I are new in town. My father thought it best for me to enroll in the fall rather than in the middle of the term."

Bill Grover nodded. "I see, I see. What's your father's name? Might be I know him."

"I very much doubt it, sir."

"It ain't Osama or Saddam, is it?"

"Sir?" Ali said, but Bill Grover, with the pep in his step of a much younger man, sauntered over to the front door and locked the deadbolt.

He turned toward Ali, teeth bared. "I want you to empty your pockets for me, boy."

"May I ask why, sir?"

"Don't be a smart-ass, you sandy motherfucker. I saw you slip some of that silverware in your pocket. Not too smart on your part, pal. I was standing five feet from you! I may be getting old, but my eyes ain't gone out on me yet." Bill Grover was practically growling. "What else you steal from me? What's under that fuckin' towel on your head?" Ali hadn't been wearing a turban; he had been wearing his usual hat, the one I saw when I first met him.

"Sir, I have not stolen anything from you or anyone before. I have no reason to start here. Silverware, you said? What is the value in that?"

The big words and the intellectual way Ali talked only pissed Bill Grover off more.

"Unlike you, that silverware is *pure,* boy! An heirloom from the Civil War." He snorted. "Value? You don't know value, huh? Well, might be I believe you. You bastards sure as hell didn't see no value in all those people you killed at the World Trade Center, did ya?"

"Sir—"

"Don't you 'sir' me." Bill Grover backed up to the front desk, his arms raised as if holding an imaginary rifle across his chest, and then he pulled the corded phone off its cradle and proceeded to dial the Pickwick Police Department's number—a number which he knew by heart despite his shoddy memory, because he was no stranger to calling the cops when a so-called "undesirable" character entered his place of business. He had done so eight times in the last six months alone.

I couldn't imagine what was going through Ali's head. It's easy for me to say that if I were him, I would've slapped the old jackass in the face with one of the spoons he accused me of stealing so the call to the police would be worth it for the guy, you know? But of course, Ali would never do anything like that. Violence was a foreign concept to him.

He could've run. *"Bill Grover"* and *"intimidating"* were not words you'd see used together in a sentence. The man was pushing seventy. He had already gone under the knife for two open heart surgeries due to a love of red meat, and he walked with a slight limp from the metal pins in his left knee (the pins were a result of a fall three winters ago, *not* from his time spent in Vietnam).

Ali stood there and waited, taking the berating words on the chin, each one chipping away pieces of his pure heart. Every subtle jab at his ethnicity sunk him lower and lower. He wanted nothing more than to be back in the familiar warmth of his home country.

And these words never stopped, not even after Ali emptied his pockets and removed his hat. Still, Bill Grover continued to insist that this fifteen-year-old boy, who happened to have a different skin tone than the majority of the people of Pickwick, was a dirty thief.

"If you didn't take the silverware, then where's it at?"

"Sir, I do not know—"

"Shut your mouth!"

Ali flinched.

The police arrived in record time—they almost

always did in small towns—and Officer Mark Cheevers dragged himself out of his cruiser. Then he reached in the cab, grabbed his hat, put it on, and sighed.

Bill Grover limped-ran toward the door, threw it open, and shouted, "In here! I got the little criminal in here, Mark!"

Cheevers, a middle-aged man with a bulging beer gut and a mustache that would've made Tom Selleck proud, was in no hurry as he crossed Center Street and lumbered around the newspaper dispensers planted on the sidewalk. He paused at the bike rack and sighed again before stepping inside Grover's Collectibles.

"How ya doin', Bill? Still crazy, I see," Officer Cheevers said.

"I ain't crazy. This little bastard tried to steal my Civil War silverware! It's *pure,* Mark! *Pure!* You know how much I can get for those? About a grand!"

He couldn't.

Officer Cheevers offered a tired smile to Ali, who couldn't stop trembling. He told me he thought he must've looked as guilty as guilty could be. All these terrible thoughts were racing through his head. Was he going to get arrested? Would his father lose his job at the gas company in Stone Park? Would his family get deported?

The officer approached, bent down a little so he was face-to-face with Ali, and sighed for the third time in less than five minutes. "Son, you look me in the eyes and tell me the truth, all right?"

Ali swallowed down the lump taking residence in his throat. "Y-yes, sir."

"Did you try to steal Mr. Grover's merchandise?"

"No, sir."

"You didn't steal none of his Civil War silverware? No spoons? Not even a knife?"

"No, sir. I emptied my pockets. I do not so much as recall seeing such items."

What he was really saying was that Bill Grover was crazy.

Luckily, Officer Cheevers, although not the best cop, knew how to read between the lines. He straightened with a grunt and said, "Well, that settles it, Bill."

"What?" Bill Grover yelped. "That's all? Can't you hook 'em up to one of those lie detector thingamajigs? I know you got one in your car, don't ya?"

"Yeah, I do," Officer Cheevers said, "and four vials of sodium pentothal. But before I stick him, I'd have to get in touch with the Pope to make sure I ain't breaking protocol, and that's a whole thing. Can't afford to get another strike on my library card, you know what I mean, Bill?"

Bill Grover nodded, as if he *did* know what the cop was saying, and a sly smile crept along Officer Cheever's lips. He turned back to Ali. "All right, son, you're free to go."

Ali didn't move—*couldn't* move.

Bill Grover slapped the front counter, rattling all kinds of junk in the showcase. "See, I knew my tax dollars was going to waste! Screw the Pope! Let's drug him and get the little bastard to tell us the truth! He's lying his teeth off! Probably even knows where that Osama is hiding!"

Officer Cheevers snorted and turned to Ali. He cocked a thumb at the door. "Go on, kid, get outta here."

"You gotta be shittin' me, Mark," Bill Grover groaned. "If you don't lock 'em up, they're gonna keep coming in here and stealing my stuff!"

"Uh-huh, I'm sure, Bill." Officer Cheevers clucked his tongue and nodded at the door again. "Chop-chop, kid."

Finally, before the policeman had a change of heart, Ali kicked himself into gear and left the store.

He bolted home, never stopping to catch his breath or check for traffic at the crosswalks.

Ten minutes later, he crawled into his bed and pulled the covers over his head like a child hiding from the monster in his closet. He said he stayed like that for an hour.

As it turned out, Ali was not home free.

Problems arose when Bill Grover, adamant about cleansing the town of anyone non-white, went down to the police department and filed a report.

The report had nothing to do with theft. It was about truancy. Grover made a big stink about the whole situation, about kids running around while they should be in school.

To appease him, the chief, a war veteran himself, and Officer Cheevers decided to make a house call to the Al-Kareems' one late afternoon.

Ali's father assured them he would enroll his son at Pickwick High as soon as possible. The police thought this was a fine idea.

After berating Ali more—though I believe his berating was with his hands and not his words—Sharif Al-Kareem kept his promise and enrolled Ali for the last quarter of the school year.

In a way, as weird as it sounds, I should be thankful for Bill Grover's racism.

Without that whole incident, Ali's father would've never put Ali in public school, and because this was where we saw each other most, Ali would never have become my best friend.

And he may have never been there to save my life that coming summer.

CHAPTER 5
BACK TO SCHOOL

CLASSES STARTED up again on January 5, 2009. As much as I wanted to not go, I absolutely had to if I didn't want to get held back a year. See, I had missed a lot of school after Owen died, and because of this I was a bit behind in a few of my classes.

Well, maybe a *bit* is an understatement.

I was technically failing about half of them when break had started, which was also the same time grades closed for the semester. The principal had granted me a two-week extension to make up what I missed, which was about a month's worth of work. Most of the teachers were reasonable about that. They offered neutered assignments and make-up tests that seemed too easy to be true.

The ones that were a little more strict—namely my Algebra II teacher, Mrs. Finch, and my English teacher, Mr. Adams—weren't throwing me any softballs. I got the same exams and essay assignments on *To Kill a Mockingbird* as all the other students. But where they were strict in that sense, they still offered me a ton of extra credit opportunities.

Mr. Adams gave me fifty bonus points for reading and answering discussion questions about this kick-ass short story by Ray Bradbury called "A Sound of Thunder." It, along with *To Kill a Mockingbird*, were about the only required reading materials I have ever actually enjoyed. I read them both during the last days of holiday break, not long after I had met and helped Ali shovel his driveway.

My mother was through the roof about the reading. She snatched the battered paperback of *Mockingbird* out of my hands one evening when she came home from work and shook it to make sure I wasn't secretly looking at a comic book or a video game manual.

"Have you gotten to the part when Boo Radley —?" she began to say.

"Hey! No spoilers, please!"

She used to do the same stuff with movies, always accidentally ruining the best bits. Not because she wanted to, but because she couldn't hold back her excitement. At that point, though, I'd probably seen more movies than her. Now when it came to books, she had me beat by a lot.

The smile that crossed my mother's face then was so warm and genuine, I still think about it to this day.

"I'm sorry. I'll leave you to it, then," she said. "But don't stay up too late, okay? You're still growing. You need sleep as much as you need knowledge!" She winked, already knowing by the determination on my face that I had no intention of falling asleep at a reasonable hour. Of course, she was right. I stayed up until four in the morning finishing that book. I was zonked the next day, barely able to keep my eyes open, but it was worth it.

So by January 4, I had just about caught up on all of my schoolwork. With time to spare too.

Principal Holden may have been a hard-ass in the disciplinary department (good luck getting out of detention if you were even five seconds late to school), but he had sons of his own and he was a big follower of Christ. Beneath that barrel chest of his lay a soft heart full of love and understanding.

So, technically, the extension he had granted me

went into effect after the break. The two weeks of vacation were for family, he said. "Rest, relax, and, even though it will be difficult, enjoy the holidays, young man."

I took his advice. Christmas was hard, yeah, but escaping through reading made it a little easier.

Books weren't all I read. I studied the local newspapers more than I had ever studied a textbook. I was looking for any incidents similar to what had happened to my brother. An animal attack, a grisly murder, a death by misadventure. There wasn't much in any of these categories, though. Most of the deaths that made headlines around here were from overdoses and robberies gone bad or domestic disputes turned deadly, and the obituaries were always full of those gone by natural causes and unfortunate accidents.

I read these articles in secret, the way a boy my age was supposed to be reading the *Playboy* magazines he had taken out of his father's closet, browsing them in the dark of my bedroom with a flashlight. I did this to not make my mother suspicious or concerned. I thought of going to the library and scouring newspapers from all over the Midwest, but as time went on, the task seemed not only daunting but a waste too. I had begun to believe Owen actually had died the way the cops said he did. And what difference did it make?

He wasn't coming back.

On the first day of the new semester, I saw the dog again.

Because it had been sixteen degrees on that January morning, my mother insisted on driving me the two miles to Pickwick High. Normally, I would've said no because she needed the extra sleep, but I'll admit that I was nervous to go back, and having my mother by my side a few minutes longer before I was cast out into the wild waters of high school again helped ease my mind.

We headed east down Whitehall Road toward Center. If you hung a left on Center and took it north for a mile and half, you'd eventually come to PHS, set far from the street to the right.

As my mother turned on her blinker at the stop sign and waited for the procession of morning traffic to pass, she breathed into her hands and rubbed them together. The heater was going full blast but only blowing out lukewarm air. That old

Chevy took a while to get going at the best of times—sixteen-degree weather was another story.

I thought I had forgotten my report on *To Kill a Mockingbird* at home, so I reached in the backseat for my book bag. Before my fingers grabbed the zipper, I caught a glimpse of something through the foggy backseat window. My heart stuttered in a way that had me thinking *heart attack*. I leaned over farther and swiped the frost and condensation away with the side of my gloved hand.

The inverted Dalmatian sat on the corner of the sidewalk, beneath the crossing green street signs for Dart and Center.

The dog was not only looking at the car but seemed to be looking right at *me*. It stayed as statue-still as it had the night I went out looking for Owen, seemingly not breathing. I noticed how no vapor clouds were drifting from its nose.

"Mom," I said shakily, sitting back in the front and pointing through her window. "Do you see that dog?"

"Huh?"

I leaned toward her as she pulled onto Center, the engine doing its normal rattle-whine that signaled Dolores Carver's arrival. Once we started puttering down the road, she glanced at where I was pointing.

"Dog? I hope not. Poor thing would freeze to death in this weather."

"You don't see it?"

"What dog, John?" She flicked her eyes at me. They were full of worry. "Are you sure you wanna go back to school today? Missing one more day won't hurt."

I barely heard the words, because when I looked back through the window, the dog was gone.

It's safe to say I did not pay much attention in my classes that first day back. My mind was fixed on the dog. Had I really seen it? Or was it a figment of my imagination, a stand-in for my lost brother or some Freudian shit like that?

I had heard our minds create these types of things to fill in the blanks after we experience trauma. Or was the dog real and my mother just missed it?

I didn't know, and I'll be honest, I was scared to find out the truth. Whatever the truth, I knew it wouldn't be good.

The new semester meant new subjects. Instead of Algebra II, English, Biology, and 3-D Art, I was somehow gifted with four blow-off classes. Because I was the new kid, I didn't get to schedule with all the other students, so I didn't get my schedule until the day of the new semester.

Someone in the guidance office had done it for me. The way they did it, I think, was by taping the classes on the wall and launching a handful of darts at them. Whatever subjects those darts landed on was what John Carver would be enrolled in. I also had a sneaking suspicion that Principal Holden overrode what the guidance office cooked up and cut me some slack schedule-wise.

In the morning I had Spanish II and American History from 1945 to Present Day. Then came the hour and a half lunch/study hall break, followed by Art and Technology and Health and Fitness, the latter class pretty much being recess for high schoolers.

I spoke decent Spanish. I had already taken the equivalent of Spanish II in Corbin my freshman year, but those credits didn't transfer as cleanly as they should have. So Spanish II was basically a repeat. I found my old workbook and wasn't surprised to see it was the exact same one we used at Pickwick High. Easy A there.

On paper, American History was the only difficult one, but my teacher was awesome. He taught more hands-on than with lectures and textbooks—or so I heard. I wasn't worried about that. Art and Technology did worry me a bit, but it turned out to be the ultimate blow-off class. Even more so than Health and Fitness, surprisingly.

In Art and Tech, we worked on digital projects using Adobe Photoshop and Illustrator. The best part was how you could check out a digital camera during class and basically roam around the school without consequences because of the hall pass around your neck.

Despite being in the second semester of the year, I was still the new kid until early March when Ali officially enrolled at Pickwick High, becoming the *new*-new kid. And as luck would have it, he wound up in my third period Art and Tech class.

Days went on like they always did. Slow, but at the same time blindingly fast. The weather got less cold —still freezing for the most part, but the snowfall was much more spaced out. Then it was March and the semester was halfway over. I woke up one weekday to a clear blue sky. Instead of thirty degrees, it was pushing fifty, and the forecast said it would be in the sixties around noon.

About time.

My mother was up, frying eggs and bacon in the kitchen. The smell was intoxicating. I shuffled past her, muttering a sleepy "Good morning" and giving her a peck on the cheek.

"A very good morning it is, honey. Your food's already on the table."

"Thanks, Mom," I said, and kissed the other cheek this time. Words can't describe how much I appreciated her.

When I got to the table, my plate was sitting in my usual spot with a paper towel draped over it, steam curling out from beneath. But my eyes focused on something else: a flyer held down by an empty glass I would eventually pour my orange juice in.

At the top of the page, in big bold letters, it read:

7th ANNUAL HARVEST FESTIVAL SHORT FILM CONTEST

"Hey Mom, what's this?" I asked.

She leaned in around the doorway. "Oh, I saw it on the bulletin board at the Lodge. Thought you'd be interested. It seems like a great opportunity for you to put that camera to use."

I scanned over the rest of the page, and when my eyes caught the bottom line, my mouth fell open.

FIRST PRIZE: $1000

That was more money than my young brain could comprehend. A thousand bucks? If I won, I'd practically be rich! But I'd never done anything more than take a picture. How the hell was I supposed to make a short film that was good enough to win a prize?

My mother came in with her own plate of steaming eggs and bacon and sat across from me.

"Eh, I don't know," I said and pushed the flyer away.

"Oh, why not? You've got that whole sketchbook full of story ideas. Why don't you turn one into a little movie?" She smiled brightly. "I could help, if you want. It would be fun!"

"None of my ideas are good. They're just copies of other movies."

"So what? That's basically how all stories are. Think about it, what's *The Lion King?*"

"Uh…a Disney cartoon?"

"It's Shakespeare's *Hamlet!*"

I went over the major plot points in my head. Prince of Denmark's father is killed by his uncle, the uncle assumes the throne and all that stuff. Kind of like Mufasa, Scar, and Simba's story, yeah. My mother was right.

"Ideas are easy," she said. "There are hardly any new ones anymore. It's all about execution. You know, putting your fingerprints on it." She started buttering her toast. *Scrape-scrape-scrape.* "I know you love those Quentin Tarantino movies—"

"Which you don't approve of."

"—but what does he do that makes you like him? Because his ideas aren't exactly new. He mishmashes a bunch of genres, and somehow it works for the general movie-going audience, right?"

"Yeah," I agreed. "And he's got style. Plus, I love the dialogue, the blood, the violence, the—"

My mother held her hand up. "Stop it, John, you're gonna make me faint."

I laughed. She was onto something here.

"Do you understand what I'm saying?" she asked. "You want to make another *Star Wars*, I say go for it. Just make it *yours*."

I picked up my fork and poked at my eggs. I suddenly wasn't too hungry. The anxiety of the *idea* of putting my stuff out there made my stomach roil.

I could feel my mother's eyes on me.

"So?" she said.

I looked up. "I'll think about it."

But I already had made up my mind, even if I wouldn't admit it right then.

I was going to do it. I was going to try and make a short film and win a thousand bucks. I'd pay my mother back for the camera, help out with the bills, and if there was enough left over, I'd go to the movie theater every day for as long as I could.

Fast forward to April and I was sixteen now. No big celebration or anything. My mother baked a homemade cake and sang me "Happy Birthday," and the only way it could've been better was if Owen had been with us.

At school, in Art and Tech, we were doing a

project in Adobe Illustrator. We had to design a poster for the school play that premiered at the end of the month. It was called *Furry Tails* and consisted of modern retellings of three classic fairy tale stories, only *all* of the characters were going to be changed to animals of a more hairy variety. The stories were: "The Princess and the Pea," "The Three Little Pigs," and "Little Red Riding Hood."

Each student was given one of the three stories to base their poster on. Mine was "The Princess and the Pea," known in the play as "The Princess and the Flea." The titular princess was a cat and the pea was a talking flea.

Ali got "Little Red Riding Hood," which had been changed to "Little Red Clopping Hoof" for the play and was about a zebra and a lion instead of a little girl and a wolf. Yeah, we were pretty sure the theater instructor, Mr. Cheville, was either on drugs or losing his mind.

After a quick demo of the ins and outs of Adobe Illustrator by Mrs. White, our ancient but jovial teacher, we were off to work. We'd come in and sit at the computer or go out and take pictures around the school to "model" our work after. As you could expect, a lot of the students checked out one of the Nikons and ditched most of the class to do nothing, but a lot stayed behind too. No one got in trouble. Mrs. White seemed to be mentally checked out but treated us like human beings and not rotten kids (like some of the teachers did). We respected her.

Ali sat across from me, our big computer monitors obscuring our faces. I leaned to the side and asked him if he wanted to be the model for my feline princess. Neither him nor I had checked out a camera yet. Me, mostly because I didn't want to go alone; and him because he'd been in the class only a few weeks. Ali looked a bit uneasy at the idea, so I told him I'd pose for Little Red Riding Hoof or the lion if he needed it.

The kid sitting beside me, a junior named Tyler, snickered and called us homos. I ignored him. That kind of thing was nothing new. Really, "homo" was mild compared to the insults the bullies slung at me back in Corbin. Ali didn't bat an eye at the term. He thought Tyler was calling him what he was—a homo sapien.

"Yes, John, I will be your cat princess," Ali said. "And you can be my Little Red Riding Hoof."

Tyler made a kissing noise. "How cute. Just wear a condom. Okay, boys?"

I gave him a thumbs-up and his laughter tapered off.

"Whatever," Tyler mumbled. "Losers."

I shrugged that one off too, and then Ali and I checked out a Nikon and signed out. The halls were desolate. Eerily quiet. My sneakers squeaked on the floor, each step excruciatingly loud.

"Where are we going?" Ali asked. He had the camera around his neck.

I tapped my chin. "I was thinking the gym. Mr. Mac seems to like me. And I know just the spot where we can get some good shots without dickheads like Tyler bothering us."

Ali nodded.

As we approached the gym, the sounds of bouncing balls echoed through the corridor. It was volleyball week in phys ed. A former college basketball player, Mr. McDonald—or Mr. Mac for short—stood about seven feet tall. His buzz cut and Adidas track suits made him look like a Russian henchman from a bad Steven Seagal movie, but for the most part he was nice enough.

I slipped in through the main entrance and jogged up to where he stood near the folded-up bleachers. He had his whistle in his mouth, and he was watching a couple of kids doing a bump, set, spike drill with the intensity of a Wimbledon line judge.

Just when I was about fifteen feet from him, a volleyball soared through the air and smacked me in the side of the face. It hit like a bomb, and I went down in a heap.

I heard a familiar voice say, "Heads up, Carver."

Rubbing my cheek, I turned and saw Ryan Kensington standing over me. His best friend Dave was a little farther behind.

Ryan had this big grin on his face and something like murder in his eyes.

An instantaneous flare of hatred sliced through my insides. Ryan was with my brother on the night he disappeared. You might remember that he had lied to the cops to save his own skin, and when Dave told the truth, Ryan got nothing more than a slap on the wrist.

"Nice form," Dave said. "Great shot."

"Eh," Ryan said. "I was aiming for his nuts. But I figured they haven't dropped yet."

With my head throbbing and my cheek burning, I saw red. I shot up and went after Ryan like a rabid dog.

I managed to get to him and grab his PICK-

WICK P.E. shirt in one hand while I raised my right fist, but before I could swing, Dave was on me. I stood no chance against him. He pulled me off Ryan with one arm as Ali sprinted toward us from the main entrance.

Ali moved like a blur. I mean, I have never seen anyone move that fast in all my life.

Dave dropped me and jumped out of the way.

A shrill whistle blew, and a crowd gathered around us, anticipating a brawl. Had he not been interrupted, I believe to this day that Ali would've torn both of their heads off.

Mr. Mac shouted, "Hey! Hey! That's enough!"

The babble from the other students had gone silent. Forgotten volleyballs bounced and rolled away from the courts. Tennis shoes no longer squeaked on the hardwood.

"Cool it! I said cool it right now!" Mr. Mac wedged himself between us.

Ryan was backing up, his hands held high, palms out. He wore a smug look of satisfaction on his face and his shirt was twisted in a wrinkled mess from me grabbing him. "I'm cool, Mr. Mac. I'm cool."

I kept my hands bunched into fists.

"We were just messing around," Dave said.

Mr. Mac looked at Ali and I. "What are you two doing in my gym?"

I was still breathing too hard and fast to give him an answer. Ali offered nothing either. His lips were tightly sealed, and he was back to his normal, mild-mannered self. But that flash of anger I saw in him…it both scared and impressed me.

Mr. Mac planted both hands on his hips and stooped down, staring at us. "Well?"

I shook my head. "We needed to ask you a question, that's all, but then Ryan pelted me with a volleyball—"

"It was an accident!" Ryan said in this over-exaggerated tone, and him and Dave started snickering. They stopped when Mr. Mac glared at them.

"Hey, I'm a football player, Mr. Mac," Ryan said. "Volleyball ain't my game."

"Take a lap, Kensington."

"But it was an accident!"

"*Now.*"

Ryan sighed, his shoulders dropped. Dave covered his mouth with one of his meaty hands, trying not to laugh.

Mr. Mac raised his eyebrows at him. "Hey, big boy, you go on ahead and join him."

"What? I was trying to break it up—"

"Go on, Rivers." Mr. Mac blew his whistle. It was a terrible noise that still haunts me to this day. "Everyone else, get back to your drills! Or you're *all* gonna be running laps! How's that sound?"

Slowly, the crowd of students dispersed, and the hollow, rubbery sounds of bouncing volleyballs filled the gym once more.

Mr. Mac put one of his large hands on my shoulder and lowered his voice. "Listen, I'm gonna let this one slide, Carver. But if I catch you in here again or picking fights with anyone else, it's detention. Not after-school detention either. I'm talking about *Saturday* detention. Got it?"

Oh, I got it. Saturday detention was about as bad as it got. See, the detention after school was only for an hour, and the teacher that stayed behind to chaperone didn't give two shits what you did as long as you were in the classroom and kept somewhat quiet. Easy-peasy.

But *Saturday* detentions… Ooh boy, those were from seven to noon, and the chaperone was a man named Mr. Holzapher, who not only resembled Hitler in his appearance (short, chubby, dark hair, and a mustache an inch or two longer than the notorious upper lip patch Adolf had sported), but orchestrated his detentions like a Nazi.

You so much as broke the mandated silence with a sneeze or a cough and Holzapher would give you another Saturday. Granted, most of what I had heard of Holzapher's notoriety was secondhand, but there's always some truth to the rumors, isn't there?

"You boys understand me?" Mr. Mac repeated, this time a bit slower.

"Yes, sir," I said.

Ali nodded.

"Good. Now, what was it you wanted to ask me?"

I figured it was pointless. I had almost gotten in a fight right in front of the guy. No way he'd ever let me do what I wanted to do, but I asked him anyway. It was worth a shot.

"I was wondering if Ali and I could take some pictures of the gymnastic mats?"

"What for?"

"An Art and Tech project."

Mr. Mac scratched his head. I could tell he wanted to say no, but I could also tell he was doing that sympathy thing that everyone else had started doing around me because of Owen. Only Mr. Mac wasn't as subtle about it as the other teachers. "Sure, but just because I liked your brother. He was a hell of an athlete."

It stung a bit. Like scratching at a barely healed wound. But I put on my most polite smile and said, "Yes, sir, he really was."

He nodded at a blue painted metal door on the far end of the court. "Mats are in the aux gym. It's a mess, but I'm sure you'll find 'em." Another scratch of his head. "Don't go fuc—*screwing* around with the equipment either. Got it?"

"Yes, sir. Thank you."

"Yeah, yeah."

Ali and I slipped into the cool darkness of the auxiliary gym. It was much smaller than the main one, which was where they played the home basketball games and held these ridiculous pep rallies almost every Friday during football season. The aux gym smelled like sweat and rubber and dust.

I found the light switches on the wall to my right. I flipped them, but only one of the large overhead lights flickered on. It gave off this buzzing sound that reminded me of a bug zapper. Probably a fire hazard, and it barely shed any light.

"It is kind of…eerie in here, is it not?" Ali said.

"I like it. Quiet, chilly, almost peaceful."

The door slammed with a *boom!* behind us, and Ali jumped, gasping. When he realized what had caused him such fright, he started laughing. I didn't laugh with him, because I was still a little shaken from what happened with Ryan and Dave.

It didn't take long for Ali to notice. "Did that Ryan Kensington hurt you in there, John?" he asked.

I put a hand on my cheek. The skin there warmed the tips of my fingers, but I felt no pain. "No. Just pissed me off. But dude, thanks for coming to help me. You didn't have to do that."

"You are my friend, and it is a friend's duty to defend said friend's honor."

I grinned. "Dude, you are so weird. But, like, in a good way."

"Why would he do that to you? To me, it did not look like an accident…it looked *calculated*," Ali said. "Are you feuding?"

I chuckled again as I found the thin blue gymnastic mats stacked in a corner besides a bunch of boxes of yellowed and cracked plastic jump ropes. I dragged them out. The floor of the auxiliary gym was spongy, because once upon a time this part of the school was used to host the wrestling meets. A failed tax levy cut a few of the less popular sports, wrestling included. So there was hardly any noise as I pulled the mats into one of the open areas. I climbed up on top of them. They sank a bit beneath my weight. The whole time I was doing this, I was thinking about Ali's question. Was there a feud between Ryan Kensington and I? That was a hard one to answer.

I cleared my throat. "You know, with Ryan and me, it's kinda complicated. I wouldn't exactly call it a feud. If it is, it's one-sided. I don't like him, I never have, but Ryan and my brother were friends…well, maybe I'm being a little generous there. I think he's a bully. That's all. And I don't like bullies."

Ali laced his fingers together and twiddled his thumbs. He wouldn't look me in the eye as he said in a small voice, "Ah, yes, about your brother…I am very sorry about that."

There was an uncomfortable fluttering in the pit of my stomach. I hadn't expected Ali to know about Owen, him being new and his father not wanting to meddle in anyone's business and all. The thing about small towns like Pickwick, though, is that secrets are hard to keep. When one person knows something, it spreads and spreads, and whether you want to hear about it or not, it gets in your head like the lyrics to an overplayed pop song.

"My father read about the memorial in the newspaper," Ali said. "I recognized your brother's surname. It was a terrible thing. May he be with Allah—er, whichever God he placed his faith in."

I chuckled. "I think the only gods my brother placed his faith in were Tom Brady and LeBron James. Maybe Hugh Hefner too. Not for my mom's lack of trying, though."

Ali nodded. I wasn't sure he knew who those people were.

"It's okay," I said. "Thanks." I reached for the camera. "Let's get these pictures taken."

We got the pictures and headed back. On the way, Ali asked me if I had any plans for the weekend. I told him I didn't, besides maybe starting work on my short film.

The deadline would be here before I knew it. Time to get off my ass.

"Film?" Ali said. "You are making a film?"

"Yeah, I love movies. My mom got me a way-too-expensive video camera."

"What kind of film is it?"

I shrugged. "Right now that's still kind of up in the air, but I'm leaning toward horror. A creature feature, if you know what that is."

"Like *Jaws*. I love *Jaws*."

I snapped my fingers. "Exactly. But *Jaws* might be setting the bar a little *too* high. I'd love to have a big animatronic shark to use. Easy to direct something that doesn't defy your orders. Sadly, my budget is thin. I've got about fifty bucks, so I'm probably not going to show anything more than a few glimpses of the creature. You know, a claw here, some glowing demon eyes there. Good thing fake blood is pretty cheap."

Ali lit up like a kid walking into a big toy store. "That sounds very fun. I would like to help."

"Help?" I tilted my head back and forth. "Well, like I said, I don't have much of a budget... meaning I can't pay you anything."

"That is okay. I do not need compensation. The enjoyment will be enough."

I chuckled. "You're a strange one, Ali Bu Ali Al-Kareem."

"I will take that as a compliment, John Carver."

I held my hand out low, the palm facing up.

Ali arched an eyebrow. Unsure of what to do, he poked my fingers.

I pulled away, laughing. "No! Gimme five, dude."

"Ah, I see." Ali nodded and eased his hand on top of mine.

Our good pal Tyler happened to be coming out of the bathroom as we passed by. He snorted, gave us a wide berth, and mumbled, "Friggin' homos."

Again, I ignored him. "What the hell is that?" I said to Ali.

"I—uh, only did what you asked."

"I said *give* me some five, not treat me like your long-lost lover in a Nicholas Sparks book."

"Forgive me, I am not familiar with any Nicholas Sparks books?"

I sighed, but I was secretly glad he didn't know about the romance author. "Just…forget I said that."

After *To Kill a Mockingbird* had ignited my newfound love of reading, I dipped into my mother's bookshelves on a slow, snowy day. First I read *The Notebook* because I recognized the title from the infamous Ryan Gosling and Rachel McAdams movie, and the next thing I knew, I had the dude's entire bibliography under my belt. Only other books I had read faster than his was the *Harry Potter* series back when I was younger.

"What I meant was," I said, "you gotta mean it when you give someone five. Here, hold out your hand again."

Hesitating slightly, Ali did, and then I smacked him a good one. A real stinger. He drew back and shook his hand like it was on fire.

I chuckled. "See? That's how it's done. You gotta *mean it.*"

"You Americans are odd."

"In the best way, though."

"If you say so."

We went back to our seats. I popped the memory card out and plugged it into the slot. Ali was standing over my shoulder as I flipped through the pictures we got, him and I in a variety of ridiculous poses that tried to predict what a cat, a zebra, and a lion would look like if they walked upright regularly.

The bell rang a few seconds later, and like a hive mind, all the students rolled their chairs away from their desks and started packing up.

"So," Ali said as we went with the crowd, "can I help? With the film?"

I thought about it for a moment. Sharing my

ideas, that was scary...but I knew there was no way I could do it by myself.

"Yeah, that'd be nice. Come over after school and I'll show you what I've got so far."

"Thank you!" He held out his hand. "Five?"

I smirked and went to slap his palm, but he pulled it away.

"Too slow," he said.

CHAPTER 6
PRE-PRODUCTION

ALI and I walked home when school let out for the day. The weather was mild, but the sun was warm.

My head was on a constant swivel, eyes peeled for the strange dog, which I hadn't seen since January. As the weather got warmer, more and more people were out and about. Lots of dog walkers.

I thought it was definitely possible I'd see the inverted Dalmatian now that spring was here (if I hadn't imagined it in the first place; I mean, c'mon, a black Dalmatian with white spots?). But I didn't see it that day.

Ali and I got to Whitehall Road in about thirty minutes. I climbed the porch steps and unlocked the door. It creaked open. I stepped aside.

"Welcome to my humble abode," I said.

The smell of a grilled cheese my mother must've made before heading off to work for the evening still hung in the air.

Ali bowed. "Thank you."

I came in after him, pulling the door shut behind us. "It ain't Wayne Manor, but it gets the job done."

Ali took it all in with wide eyes and a happy smile on his face. "It is wonderful."

"Thanks…but it's not."

"Yes, it is. It seems like an actual *home*. There are pictures on the walls, shoes and coats in the closet. And the furniture looks as if someone has sat in it!" His smile faltered. "My current house…it is quite, how you say, sterile?"

"That's okay. You just moved here, man. Give it time, you and your dad and brother will make it your own."

"No, I do not think so. It seems neither are ever home, and when they are, they are sleeping or arguing." He sighed. "I miss my mother and my sisters."

"Sorry to hear that. Are they coming out here anytime soon?"

"That is the goal, but we will see." Ali shook his

head as if to shake some of the sadness away. "Now, please, tell me about this film."

I let out a nervous laugh. "Follow me."

I guided him to the second floor of our Cape Cod. Depending on the season, the temperature rose or dropped about two degrees the higher you went. The place had central heating and cooling, but the upstairs never got the memo.

It was freezing in the winter and hotter than hell in the summer. Even on this early spring day that sat somewhere in the sixties, I was getting a preview of the heat to come.

There was a small bathroom at the top of the steps. I mean, seriously small. I couldn't squat on the toilet without my knees bumping the tub or the sink cabinet. And if you went right, you'd run into a closed door. That was Owen's room.

On the outside of the door was a hook, and hanging there was Owen's varsity jacket from Corbin. Any time I looked at it, I got sad. Sad because he'd never wear it again, sad because he'd never get one from Pickwick High.

It was a damn shame, man.

My mother hadn't yet touched any of his stuff; I had a feeling she wouldn't for years.

Go left and you'd find my room. Posters were

my wallpaper. I had everything from *Star Wars* to *Twelve Angry Men* covering every inch of the wood paneling. A rug with a design like the hotel carpet in *The Shining* lay between my bed on the right and my tiny desk on the left.

There was a plastic dresser at the foot of my bed, the drawers half-open, socks and underwear hanging out of them like guts out of a Romero zombie. I pushed the light switch and then pulled the cord to start the overhead fan. The breeze was welcoming.

"Sorry for the mess." I scooted some junk beneath my bed with the side of my Nike.

"It is no problem," Ali said. "I have seen much worse from my older brother."

"Sounds like him and me would get along." I chuckled as I slid into the cheap computer chair at my desk. It popped like a crackling spine.

From a drawer, I pulled out my notebook and opened it to a page of scribblings that no one but me could decipher. "You ready?"

Ali nodded, and I began.

After about twenty minutes of me ranting and Ali listening with his utmost attention, I closed the notebook and said, "Well, what do you think?"

Ali scratched his chin. "I like it…"

"There's a 'but' coming here, isn't there?"

"How will I play a female character? Jamie, her name was, yes?"

"Yeah. Jamie Cameron."

The name was supposed to be a double homage. First to my personal favorite scream queen, Jamie Lee Curtis, and second to one of my favorite directors, James Cameron.

I envisioned her as a gorgeous blonde, one of the most popular seniors at Haddon High School (as in Haddonfield, another nod to *Halloween* and Jamie Lee Curtis). Hey, cut me a little slack, I was a teenager. I guess I didn't know much about nuance back then.

"Can you change the main character to a male? That would better suit me."

I raised my eyebrows. "As hilarious as it would be to see you in a blonde wig, I wasn't thinking you'd be the star of the film, Ali. No offense. I was thinking more like you could be the stand-in for the little glimpse of the monster I show, all that subtle stuff, as well as maybe Jamie Cameron's boyfriend."

"The one who gets ripped apart in the fourth scene?"

"Bingo."

Ali grinned. "Okay, I am not wholly against that. No one is a leading man right out of the gate, are they?"

"Nope. Gotta build up to it. Do the grunt work. The main character has to be a girl anyway. It's, like, a given in horror movies. Final Girls are a thing. Ellen Ripley in *Alien*, Laurie Strode in *Halloween*, Sidney Prescott in *Scream*, and on and on."

"Perhaps Jamie Cameron can be on that list someday."

"That would be a dream," I said.

"Who will play her?"

I shrugged.

"Have you contacted those in the drama department at school? I am sure you can find a talented actress there."

"I haven't. You know, talking to girls is kind of… hard. I had a person in mind when I wrote Jamie Cameron, but—no, never mind. That's stupid."

"Who?"

"You probably don't know her. She's a senior. Not a cheerleader, but still probably like one of the most popular girls in school. She's in theater too. I'm pretty sure she's in the *Furry Tails* play. Her name's Becca Tanner."

"Whoever she is, she is just human like us, John."

"On paper, sure. But even if I could muster up the courage to talk to Becca, she's not really the one I'm worried about."

"Who are you worried about?"

I slouched. "Her friends. She hangs out with Ryan Kensington. You know, the asshole who beamed me with a volleyball today. They might even be dating…or banging, I dunno, not sure. But I'd have no shot."

"Perhaps it is best to look for someone else."

"Perhaps." We sat there in silence for a moment until I shrugged and said, "Screw it, we'll worry about who to cast later. You and me can get started without a main character. This is still pre-production. We nail that, we nail the filming. There's lots of establishing shots I want to get. Monster shots. Even some shots of Jamie's boyfriend. It's only April. We've got time."

"That is the spirit, John!"

We slapped each other five, and then I introduced Ali to the world of Master Chief and *Halo 3* on my Xbox 360. The gaming didn't stop until the sun went down and Ali had to get home.

It was the first time in a long time where I felt happy. Like actually happy.

My hope in the short film contest was renewed by Ali's enthusiasm.

On Monday, I brought my notebook to school with me so he and I could go over it in Art and Tech. We had turned the auxiliary gym into our own office of sorts during third period.

There, for about two weeks, we ran through the dialogue of my script, putting on voices for the characters and laughing our asses off at how ridiculous we sounded. We storyboarded, we tested monster makeup I bought from Party City, sketched character wardrobes, and brainstormed about a million working titles that neither of us could agree on.

We pretty much did everything but our actual schoolwork.

Then one day near the end of April, my enthusiasm was shattered. I was waiting in line for lunch by myself—Ali had left early for a dentist appointment but would be back for third period—and Becca Tanner and her friends were standing a few spots ahead of me.

I was staring at her, but not for the reasons a teenage boy usually stares at the prettiest girl in school. I was staring at her because I was trying to think of ways I could approach and ask her to be in the movie.

Getting her to star in my short film, I believed, was the difference between winning the contest and getting laughed out of the Harvest Festival.

And okay, yeah, maybe I was kind of checking her out too.

Becca wore a tight pair of jeans and a low-cut blouse. Her naturally tan skin stood out against the white belt around her waist. A waterfall of silky blonde hair fell almost to her butt.

She was huddled around two other beautiful girls and a trio of guys wearing their varsity jackets. They were talking animatedly and laughing, not a care in the world for any of them.

Only when Ryan Kensington cut the line, coming up behind Becca and wrapping his arms around her, did I look away. It was almost at this exact moment, someone nudged me in the back.

"Why don't you just take a picture, weirdo?"

I didn't know who it was. Some skinny kid with a buzzcut and meanness in his eyes. I stumbled forward, lost my footing, and splayed out on the cold floor. My notebook went flying out of my hands.

The skinny kid and his friends laughed harder. I heard the general clamor in the rotunda grow quieter as most everyone stopped and waited to see what would happen next.

It is rare to hold the attention of a bunch of hyperactive high schoolers for long, but one thing that's guaranteed to have them completely engrossed is a potential fight.

I had no fight in me, though.

Instead, I raced for my notebook before someone got ahold of it. Reading the character descriptions and backstories would be like reading my personal diary.

I'm pretty sure there were a few poems in there too. Real dark teenage angst stuff that makes my cheeks red to this day.

"What the hell is this?" Ryan Kensington said.

Slowly, I craned my head up and saw I was too late. I got to my feet and mumbled, "Thanks," to Ryan as I reached for the notebook.

He whirled away from me.

"Can I have that back? Please," I said.

"'*Jamie Cameron is a gorgeous blonde senior with long legs and the body of a goddess. Like Becca Tanner,*'" Ryan read from one of the pages. He held it up so everyone could see what I had sketched. My artistic ability wasn't great, but it was good enough to see I had obviously drawn a slightly exaggerated version of Becca Tanner.

Speaking of her, Becca's eyes widened. She let out an exaggerated gasp and snatched the notebook from Ryan.

My stomach dropped to my toes. I could've fainted.

"Is that—is that supposed to be me?" she said.

I stuttered. What the hell was I supposed to say? I didn't know, so I just chuckled awkwardly.

One of the girls near Becca leaned over and looked at the picture. "Oh my God, that's *so* weird," she said.

"It's not her," I said. "It's just a stupid drawing."

"A drawing of *my* girlfriend," Ryan stepped forward, his hands curling into fists.

I flinched and tried to prepare for a punch to the face, although you can never really prepare to get punched. "You keep Becca out of your little jerk-off fantasies. You hear me?" He ripped the page out, crumpled it, and tossed my notebook.

Someone in the crowd shouted, "You gonna let him talk to you like that, New Kid?"

Yeah, I guess I was.

I rushed toward my notebook, grabbed it, and ran out of the rotunda, trying not to think about the everyone in there laughing at me.

What a fucking day.

"Smooth move at lunch," Tyler said as I sat down at my desk in Art and Tech. "Guess you're not as gay as I thought you were. But c'mon, dude, Becca Tanner?" He laughed. "Dream big."

Ali walked in, smiling, and pointed to his freshly cleaned teeth. He pulled his chair out and lowered his voice. "What is this about Becca Tanner?"

"Nothing," I said. "Movie's off."

"What? Why?"

"Just forget it."

I eventually told Ali about the incident. He shrugged it off in his normal Ali way and encouraged me not to quit, but I was dead set on scrapping the project.

I couldn't handle any more embarrassment. I figured I'd return my camera and buy myself an axe. You know, get started on my career as a lumberjack.

School dragged on for another few weeks. I did my best to avoid Ryan Kensington, and especially Becca Tanner. I was a master at that, although I would occasionally get tripped walking down the hallway or have my books slapped out of my hands by one of their friends.

Then came May, and the seniors graduated. For us underclassmen, school didn't let out for the summer until early June. Still, I didn't have to worry about running into them anymore. That was nice.

Miraculously, I managed decent grades. My mother was happy about that, but she kept asking me about the short film contest. I didn't have the heart to tell her I had decided to give up.

My go-to answer to this question was, "I'm working on it, Mom." Then she'd smile and tell me she couldn't wait to see it. Like clockwork.

May gave way to June, and finally I was free

from the prison of Pickwick High for three months. Ali and I walked out the door together. In the parking lot, his father's old Mercedes idled.

Mr. Al-Kareem waved Ali over. They were going to the airport to pick up Ali's other brother and uncle—both who managed to get jobs at the same gas company. Slowly but surely, his whole family was moving to the United States. Come August, his mother and two sisters would be here, and Ali was over the moon about that.

"Good luck," I said.

"Thank you, friend. Would you like to play basketball tomorrow?"

Since the weather was mostly beautiful now, he and I had started going to a nearby park and shooting around when we had the chance.

"Yeah, if it's nice out."

We did our handshake, which had evolved from a simple high-five to a low-five, where our palms slid over one another and finished with a fist bump. Then he was off.

I would have to ring in the start of summer vacation by myself, but at least it was warm and sunny, the nicest day I could remember since the summer before.

I unlocked my bike from the rack and took off.

A cool breeze brought on the smell of freshly cut grass and ruffled my hair from my brow. It was only in the seventies, but the sun beat down deliciously on my bare arms.

On Center Street near the business section, the sidewalks were crowded, so I stuck to the road. The longer I pedaled, the more it felt like all my problems, all my worries, fell away from me.

Loose coins jingled in my pocket. I didn't have to buy lunch thanks to Mrs. White throwing us a pizza party in Art and Tech instead of handing out a final exam.

With this extra money, I decided I'd treat myself to an ice cold pop from the hardware store on the corner of Center and Elkwood. It was called Pierce's Hardware Depot, and the only reason a kid like me would go near a place like that was because they had a Coke machine near the front entrance.

The Cokes came in glass bottles and only cost you a dime. I planned on grabbing two, and maybe a pack of Reese's from the checkout counter. Treat myself, you know.

I turned left, hopped the curb, and leaned my bike up against the wall. No one was at the vending machine, but a steady flow of people were going in and out of the store.

I pulled out the change from my pocket and rummaged through it, looking for a dime in a sea of pennies and quarters, when I heard a young woman's voice close behind me.

"Hey, John, right? John Carver?"

My heart didn't bother dropping. It about shriveled up and died. Because this voice belonged to Becca Tanner. I turned around with no idea what to say or do.

Run? Scream? Both?

"You okay?" Becca's blonde hair was tied back in a tight ponytail. A white apron with *Pierce's* written across the middle pocket hung over the cargo pants and red polo shirt she wore.

"Uh…um…I—" I raised a hand and smiled. At least I thought I smiled. I can't imagine I looked very flattering. "I'm not stalking you, I swear. I had no idea you worked here—"

She laughed. "Relax, John."

"Holy shit, she actually knows my name," I whispered, and then I realized I had said that out loud and my cheeks turned a scorching red. "Shit…" I slapped my forehead and rubbed my temples. "I mean, not *shit*."

"*Not shit?*" Becca repeated.

"Yeah, uh, I know it's not polite to swear in

front of ladies. My mother always says that, at least. But then she goes around and curses all the time when she thinks no one's around—" I slapped my forehead again. "Okay, I'm just gonna shut up now."

"Yeah…cool. So, I'm glad I caught you here," she said. I opened my mouth to say something—I don't know what, but it was probably something stupid. Thankfully, Becca kept talking. "I wanted to apologize for that time at lunch. Ryan, he's protective. I mean, he's a jerk sometimes, but he was just trying to, like, defend my honor or some bullshit."

"Oh, it's cool," I said. "No hard feelings."

"But you're not, like, really obsessed with me or anything, are you?"

"Define obsessed." I chuckled.

"Um…"

"Sorry. That was a joke. No, I'm not obsessed with you. I swear."

"Okay, good," she said.

I stepped aside as an elderly couple walked past us through the automatic double doors.

"Yeah, no," I went on, looking back at Becca. "I was going to enter in the Harvest Festival's short film contest and you were my first choice to play the lead character. That's all that was. Out of context, yeah, I can see how it was weird. I'm sorry."

"Interesting," Becca said.

"With your drama background and charisma, I thought you'd be perfect. You killed it in the school play, by the way."

She smiled. "Thank you."

I nodded.

"So who'd you get to play the part?"

I tilted my head. "What?"

"For the short film?"

"Oh. No, I decided not to do it."

"Why?"

I shrugged. "I don't know. I was way out of my comfort zone, I guess. That, and no budget." I looked over her head at the stream of traffic going down Center Street. "Would've been nice to win that thousand bucks, though."

Becca's eyes lit up. "That's the prize?"

"Yeah."

"Are you crazy?" She pushed me playfully on the shoulder. I wasn't prepared for that, and I stumbled back like she was the strongest person in the world.

"What?"

"You're making that movie, John."

"I am?"

"Yes, and I'm gonna be your lead."

"You are?"

"Yep, if you share the prize money."

It suddenly felt like the earth had stopped spinning. Was I dreaming?

"Fifty-fifty?" she asked.

"You can have it all," I said.

"No. I couldn't do that. But five hundred would definitely help. I'm trying to get out of this crappy town." She held out her hand. "We have a deal?"

"Don't you wanna know what it's about, the short film?"

"Doesn't matter. I'll knock it out of the park regardless," Becca said. She nodded at her hand. "Deal?"

I shook her hand. "Deal."

I could've jumped with joy and screamed at the top of my lungs, but I was trying to stay cool. Not to mention a million thoughts were storming through my mind.

"Okay, deadline is the end of August. That gives us close to three months. It's only going to run about twenty minutes, but—"

"Deep breath, John. We'll make it happen."

"Holy shit, I gotta tell Ali."

"The foreign kid?"

"Yeah, he's helping. Doing technical stuff and playing the monster, and maybe your boyfriend…if you're okay with that?"

"Wait, the monster?"

"Yeah. It's a horror movie."

Now she was going to back out, and my hopes would be crushed. I knew it was too good to be true.

"Sick," she said. "I love horror movies."

"Really?"

"Hell yeah. When do we start?"

I blinked, at a loss for words.

"Hello? Earth to John."

"Uh, tomorrow night? If you're not busy."

"I'll make sure I'm not," she said. "That'll be easy. I was supposed to hang with Ryan, but he's been a real dickhead ever since I told him I planned on going to California. Like, whatever. He's going to Ohio State anyway. He doesn't need me." She waved her words away. "Sorry. Yeah, tomorrow. Where at? Your place?"

My place? I stopped myself from pinching my arm. If this was a dream, I didn't want to wake up.

"Yes? No?" Becca said.

I remembered Owen telling me the key with

girls—the key to life—was confidence. If you looked and acted like a bumbling idiot, no one would take you seriously.

I blinked and gave a slight shake of my head. "Uh, yeah. *Yes.* Tomorrow night, say around nine? It has to be dark."

"Where do you live?"

"Pickwick. 6856 Pickwick Lane. It's not far from Sunny Park."

"I know the street."

"Thank you," I said. "Really."

"No big deal. You should've just asked me, though," she said. "I don't bite."

I chuckled.

"I gotta go clock in now." She rolled her eyes. "Lord help me."

I raised a hand and waved. "Have fun."

I picked up my bike and headed for the sidewalk. As I rolled across the small parking lot, Becca called after me.

"Hey! John!"

I stopped, turned around. "Yeah?"

"What's the movie gonna be called?"

A tornado of working titles spun through my brain—*One Night Death, The Kill, Last Breath*—and I rejected them all.

Inspired, my hope renewed, the Goddess of Creativity suddenly whispered in my ear. All I did was repeat it.

"*Creature,*" I said. "It's gonna be called *Creature.*"

I called Ali when I saw his father's car back in the driveway later that evening.

"Code Red," I told him. "We got a major Code Red."

"I am not familiar with this *code,*" he said. There was excited talking in the background. Someone yelled at Ali in Arabic.

"It's a big deal," I said. "The movie's back on."

"Really?"

"Yes. And Becca Tanner's on board."

"You are lying."

"I'm not."

Ali shouted, "Yes!" which was promptly followed by more harsh-sounding Arabic thrown his way and him replying too fast for me to even begin to understand.

"I know you're busy, so I'll explain later," I said. But she's coming over tomorrow night, and I'll need your help."

"I will be there."

"Ali," I said. "We got our Jamie Cameron."

"We got our Jamie Cameron!" he repeated a little too loudly.

Becca showed up at about 9:30 the next night. Ali and I had cleaned up real nice, both ourselves and the house.

I burned one of my mother's candles, a lemony scented one, and the whole place smelled like summer.

The only problem was I had nicked myself shaving. I had never shaved before, and to be honest, I didn't have much *to* shave, but I figured better safe than sorry.

Ali shaved often. He was especially hairy for how old he was. He tried to show me how to do it, and of course, I messed up. So I had this big glob of drying blood on my neck.

"You can hide it with a bandage," Ali said. "Perhaps Becca will think you are tough when she sees it."

We were in the tiny bathroom upstairs. I was soaking sheet after sheet of toilet paper red. "Go ahead and open that drawer right there, Ali. Pull out the Band-Aids and tell me with a straight face that a girl would ever think wearing one of those was tough."

Ali grabbed the box and held it up. He started laughing. "Mickey Mouse? Okay, yes, you have a fair point there."

"My mother thinks they're cute."

"Perhaps Becca will too."

"No. It'll stop bleeding soon. I hope." I wet a washcloth and cleaned up the smeared blood on my neck. "And it's not like she's coming over for a date. She's coming over to work on the movie."

"Given the way you have spruced up, you could have fooled me."

I frowned. "Is it the cologne? Too much?"

"Well, it is a bit…strong."

"Shit." I rushed into my room and switched my polo for a clean t-shirt right as the doorbell rang. "Shit! Shit! She's here!"

"Deep breath, John," Ali said. "Remember, she is a human like us." He patted me on the back and headed downstairs.

I followed him. I was nervous as hell.

Ali opened the door. There stood Becca Tanner on my porch, still in her work uniform, looking like the most beautiful girl in the world. She was chewing bubblegum and staring at us.

The heat from outside drifted in with the sounds of chirping crickets and the smell of summer.

"You gonna invite me in or what?" Becca said. She blew a large bubble and popped it with her tongue. The sound it made snapped me back to reality.

In hindsight, we must've seemed like the biggest dweebs of all time. Two scrawny teenagers, one with gel in our hair, his face sloppily shaved, smelling like an explosion at an Axe Body Spray factory.

"Oh, yeah, come in, come in," I said, stepping aside.

Becca looked around, taking it all in. "Nice place," she said. "It's like I've walked inside of a lemon."

I chuckled nervously and made a mental note to blow out the candle burning on the mantle when she turned her back.

"Becca, this is Ali—"

"Ali Bu Ali Al-Kareem," he finished. He stuck out his hand, and Becca took it, but instead of a common shake, he bowed and brought her hand to his lips, kissing it gently. "I am enchanted to officially make your acquaintance, Becca Tanner."

Becca stared at him for a solid minute, her eyes wide. I was pretty sure she was going to smack him, or maybe call Ryan over to come kick his ass. Miraculously, she did neither.

She just said, "Okay, that was…*weird*. I'm okay with pretending that never happened."

"Me too," I said.

Ali was unbothered, and to be fair, I envied him for his confidence.

"Well, everything's set up on the dining room table. You ready to see what you signed up for?"

"You know it," Becca said as she and Ali followed me through the living room down the short hallway and into the dining room.

I had laid out a few copies of the script, a storyboard of note cards, wardrobe ideas, and a shooting schedule Ali and I cooked up a few hours earlier.

We went over the story for about half an hour. That's all it took, really. I guess I had vastly overestimated the amount of prep we'd need.

Now all three of us were sitting at the table in silence. I twiddled my thumbs, avoiding eye contact with Becca. I found her beauty almost painful.

Ali had no problem, though. He was beaming at

her. I kicked him under the table. He jumped and said, "Ow! Why did you strike me?"

"What?"

"You kicked me, and I find that quite rude, John."

"Nope. I didn't kick you." I looked at him with wide eyes.

He wasn't getting the message.

He bent down and rubbed his shin, wincing. "You most certainly did. I am going to bruise from that. Why would you assault someone you call a friend?"

I looked uncomfortably at Becca.

She smiled and turned to Ali. "Dude, he kicked you because you're over here staring at me like I'm a piece of meat and you're a starving dog. It was John's not-so-subtle way of trying to keep your hormones in check."

"Was I staring?"

"Yeah, man, you were."

"I apologize, Becca," Ali said. "Your beauty is nothing short of breathtaking."

"Well, thanks. I appreciate that. But"—she shook her head—"not a chance. Neither of you."

I began fidgeting and stammering, "Of course not—no. Yeah, we're just—"

"Professional," Ali said. "We will keep this professional, yes. I am sorry."

Becca waved her hand. "It's fine. I'm used to it. I get way worse at work. The old dudes that come into the hardware store never leave me alone."

"Gross," I said.

"I tell them I'm still in high school and it's like they turn into sharks that just got a whiff of fresh blood. I can't wait until I'm outta there, and *here*. This damn town." She got up from the table. "Which is why we gotta win this thing." Her bracelets clanging together on her wrist, she brought a hand down on the script. The sudden *bang* made both Ali and me start. "So let's do it."

"Now?" I asked, swallowing the lump in my throat.

That was the hard thing about anything you did, wasn't it? The starting. I knew it, but still I hesitated. You know why? Because you couldn't fail if you never started. But Owen once told me if you never start, you'll look back in a few years and you'll realize how much not starting *was* the failure.

"Yeah, *now*," Becca said. "I'm assuming the filming part is gonna be easy. The hard part will be putting the finished product together. Editing, adding effects, and all that nerdy tech stuff. And seeing as how it's already June, the clock is ticking. Summer'll be over before we know it."

"She's right," I said. "Let's do it."

"We can probably knock the shoot out in a week or two, right?" Becca said. "With how much planning you did, maybe even less."

Ali walked into the living room, his head down. At the bay window, he parted the curtains, giving us a clear look at the sleepy stillness of Whitehall Road. "John...I can't stay much longer. In fact, I really should be getting home. My father, he wakes up often in the night to relieve his bladder. If he happens to find me out of bed, I am going to be in trouble—"

"Sometimes you gotta risk it for the biscuit," Becca said.

"Pardon?"

"He doesn't know a lot of slang yet," I said. "What she's saying is that—"

"A hot chick is asking you to break curfew, Ali," Becca interrupted. "That's about as simple as I can put it."

"But you are asking me to break curfew for the making of a short film, not anything related to sexual activities."

"'*Sexual activities*,'" Becca repeated. "Christ,

where did you get this robot? He talks like C-3PO." Becca then pulled an imaginary trigger at me and made a sound like water spraying from a sprinkler. "Down, boy. Yes, I know *Star Wars*. My dad was a geek like you two."

"*Was?*" Ali asked.

"Yeah, he's dead. The one I'm trying to make to you is that no, we're not banging, but you'll automatically gain, like, a million cool points by hanging out with me."

"How would anyone know?" I asked. I wasn't worried about being popular—I was worried about Ryan finding out and kicking my ass. He was exactly the kind of guy who would do that too.

Becca winked. "I'll put in a good word for you both. Trust me. And when we win that prize, everyone'll see our names in the credits. Duh."

Ali and I both nodded.

"Let us begin, then," Ali said.

Surprisingly, we all got along well that first night of filming. I filmed a hell of a lot of footage too. Really good stuff.

Becca was a natural. She played a frightened yet

strong heroine as if she'd been doing it her whole life.

Here's the gist of the story: Becca's character Jamie is house-sitting for some neighbors down the street who are out of town on a summer vacation.

Her boyfriend comes over, Xavier (Ali). Here, we get to know Jamie and how nice and bubbly she is. Having forgotten his phone, the boyfriend goes to his car to get it, and then BAM! something *gets* him.

After a while, Jamie goes to investigate, she finds evidence of foul play (blood and slime and all that), she goes to call the cops but the power cuts out, then this creature stalks her through the house, she fights it, and she wins.

That's the movie.

The submissions were limited to twenty minutes. You can't pack a lot of story and character development in such a short time, so I figured I'd keep it bare bones, try to speak to the audience's base instincts while trying to also make it scary as hell.

That first night we filmed the part where Xavier gets taken and Jamie goes out to investigate why he is taking so long.

And...action.

Jamie Cameron opens the front door and looks out into the dark night.

It's quiet, not even the crickets are chirping—although a few cars had gone down the street during filming, one of which was blasting bass-thumping rap music, but I'd edit that out in post-production.

We see Xavier's car (Becca's Honda Accord) parked slightly crooked at the end of the driveway, as if some great force has moved it.

The driver's side door is ajar, the inside dome light is on, casting enough light to see *something* near the back tire.

Jamie walks closer, each step more hesitant than the first.

We zoom in on her face to show the terror.

"Xavier?" she says quietly as she approaches.

Sudden stop. A *gasp*.

She covers her mouth with both hands, holding back a scream.

Zoom in on a sneaker sticking out from behind the back driver's side tire. (My old and dirty K-Swiss.)

"Xavier?"

Jamie rushes over to him.

Slowly, we follow her with the camera.

Cut.

I had to get a chair to stand on. Ali brought it to me and I climbed above Becca to film over her shoulder.

Action.

The sneaker is not connected to anything, but in the faint light there is fresh *red* liquid on it.

Jamie says, "Xavier, if this is a joke, it's not funny at all!"

But there's confusion on her face. Xavier's not like that, he's a straight shooter. Practical jokes aren't his thing. He often shrugs off the juvenile pranks his friends are so fond of pulling and shakes his head at their immaturity.

See, Xavier plans to attend Duke, and then law school, and then he'll get a nice cushy job at his father's law firm. His whole life is planned out.

Only…everyone has a plan until they're attacked by an inhuman monster, right?

Jamie picks up the shoe. "Xavier, please!"

That's when she hears it—the first low rumbling growl of the titular *Creature.*

Cut.

In reality we had a stand-in for the noise. The terrifying growl I had imagined in my head would have to be added in post, but Ali lent his voice to help. And he made maybe one of the weirdest noises I'd ever heard.

Becca wasn't able to stay in character. She cracked up, and then I cracked up with her.

"What the hell was that?" she asked.

Ali held up the shooting script, smacked it with the back of his hand. "I am only following the cues. It says '*The monster growls*' right here."

"It sounded like when Scooby-Doo does that *ruh-roh* thing mixed with a Zebra in labor," Becca said.

Bent over and practically wheezing, I had to wipe my eyes. "Dude—dude, c'mon, I can't—"

Ali shrugged. "I am only doing my job! And how do you know what a zebra sounds like when in labor? That is the real question here!"

For a solid five minutes, none of us could stop laughing.

Once we calmed down, we tried another take or two, but Becca kept smiling when she wasn't supposed to, and I couldn't hold the camera straight.

I called it for the night.

It was already going on one in the morning, which meant my mother would be home any minute now, and I really didn't want to have to explain to her why I had a girl over at the house *way* past curfew. Or risk embarrassment via her calling me "*Pookie-bear*" or something like that.

"You good to shoot more tomorrow?" I asked Becca as she was getting into her Accord. "I think it's gonna be a full moon. It'll be perfect for some of the scenes we need."

"I'll be here."

"Awesome, thank you," I said.

"Yeah, I had fun." She shifted the car into reverse. "Now don't stay up too late, boys."

With that, she backed out of the driveway and left us. Ali and I just kind of stared at each other awhile, both of us in awe. There was no way this had really happened.

Ali said, "She is quite nice. I like her."

"Yeah, me too."

But to tell you the truth, I more than liked her.

I was pretty sure I was falling in love.

CHAPTER 7
THE FULL MOON

THAT SATURDAY NIGHT, June 6, the moon was full and the skies were clear like the weather report had predicted.

My camera was fully charged, and I had a good idea of what and where I wanted to film that night. My confidence was at an all-time high.

The doorbell rang at 9:20. I looked through the peephole and got a fish-eyed view of Ali. He was wearing his usual robe and round cap. The robe was called a dishdasha, and although it was long-sleeved and fell to his ankles, the material was thin enough to keep him cool. Same for the cap, which was called a Kuma.

That night wasn't Middle East hot, but it was a hot one nonetheless.

Ali raised a hand and said, "I apologize for my tardiness."

"You're ten minutes early, dude."

"That is true, but my family believes in arriving a quarter of an hour before we are due."

"So, first ones at the party?"

"What party?"

"Never mind," I said, rolling my eyes. "But really, you don't need to put up that Golden Boy act around me, okay? I won't tell your dad."

Ali opened his mouth and then shook his head. "I— What do you mean by 'Golden Boy act?'"

"I mean, we're a couple of teenagers. We're supposed to have fun, you know?"

"Well, I do enjoy myself from time to time."

"Oh yeah? Really?" I said. "When's the last time you enjoyed yourself besides last night?"

Ali took off his hat and picked at the embroidery, thinking. "Um…"

"Yeah, exactly. See what I mean?" I put a hand on his shoulder. "Your dad isn't here. It's okay to have fun every once and awhile."

"I suppose you're right. However—"

"Ali, dude, we're not doing drugs or robbing banks. We're just hanging, so relax a little. You're only fifteen, but I swear you keep acting like this and you're gonna have a heart attack before you're thirty."

He stared at me. I could tell he was considering my words. "I'm not trying to offend you or change you or whatever. In the end, you are who you are, but life's a lot better when you're not worrying about what everyone thinks about you."

As if I was one to talk. I worried about what the bugs thought of me.

I grabbed Ali's arm and pulled him into the living room. "Here, I want you to try something for me, okay?"

Ali hunched his shoulders. "Um, all right?"

"I want you to stand on the couch and shout a bad word as loud as you can."

"What? A bad word?"

"Yeah, man. Like 'fuck' or 'shit' or 'dickhead.' I dunno, something. You sound like a British butler all the time."

"English is not my native language. I am often worried I will mispronounce a word or confuse the meanings of two and make a fool of myself—"

"Dude, I do that all the time, and I've been speaking English since I could talk. It happens. That's the way things go. No big deal. No one's gonna throw you to the sharks if you call a tomato a *toe-may-ter* or something."

Ali mouthed the latter and a smile curled the corners of his lips.

"So go on, Ali. Shout it out!"

"I am not sure if that is exactly proper."

"It's not…in most situations. But I see no reason *not* to here. My mom's not home and your dad's like a block away. Just trust me, man, it'll make you feel better."

He remained slouched, his eyes darting around the room.

"Here, I'll do it first," I said.

In my untied sneakers, I jumped up on the couch (my mother would've probably killed me if she knew about this), I raised my arms above my head, and I shouted, "FUCK!" at the top of my lungs. It was so loud, a nearby dog started barking.

Ali's mouth fell open.

"See?" I said. "Easy."

"This is a bad idea, I know it."

"Maybe," I said. "But what's life without bad ideas?"

"Safe," he said. I frowned at him, and he threw his arms up. "Fine."

Ali untied his shoes. I tried to tell him not to

bother but didn't want to kill the momentum. Then he climbed up on the easy chair in the corner of the room. It rocked unsteadily, and he stuck out his arms, grabbed the headrest, and regained his balance.

I was nodding. "Go on, man. Do it. You got this."

He inhaled deeply, closed his eyes, and screamed, "ASS-CLOWN!"

I scrambled to cover my ears at the shrillness of his voice. When I looked at Ali, he was laughing. It was like an invisible weight (more like the invisible hand of his father) had left him. And I started laughing with him.

"Ass-clown?" I said. "What the hell is that?"

He shrugged. "I do not exactly know. A man called my father that at the airport after a dispute over a parking spot."

"Well, it's creative, I'll give 'em that. Do you feel better?"

Ali grinned. "To be honest, John, I feel like I could take on the world."

I nudged him with my elbow. "See? Told ya."

Becca showed up a little after our cursing session. She wasn't in her work outfit, but wore a pair of short-shorts and a loose tank top. She held a plastic grocery bag full of the clothes she'd worn during yesterday's filming.

"Mind if I change here?"

"Y-yeah, go ahead. Bathroom is down there past the kitchen."

"Huh?" she said and gripped the hem of her tank top with both hands. She pulled her shirt up high enough for Ali and I to get a glimpse of her pierced belly button.

I shielded my eyes and spun around. "Holy sh—"

Ali hadn't, so I snagged his sleeve and yanked him back.

Becca started laughing. "Ahh, got ya!"

My face hot with embarrassment, I said, "Good one."

———

The three of us walked down Whitehall to Dart, where midway down the street, a winding path would take you through the woods and into Sunny Park.

The path was located between the Thompsons' house and another identical in design but painted a baby blue instead of white.

The Thompsons' car was in the drive, but there wasn't a single light on inside behind the drawn curtains. The grass was also a little overgrown. I found that uncharacteristic of Mr. Thompson, who took major pride in landscaping his property.

I wondered if they had gone on another vacation. They were always taking these weekend trips to see family in neighboring states. I guess Mary Thompson had a lot of family out of town.

Mary Thompson wasn't as friendly as her husband. She never smiled and always looked sick whenever I saw her, but she baked the best chocolate chip cookies I've ever had so her lack of warmth got a pass from me.

I often wondered if she suffered from some sickness Mr. Thompson didn't want to disclose to the neighborhood kid who helped him with little odd jobs every once and awhile. Cancer, maybe.

I eventually settled on the Thompsons having packed it in for an early night. They were middle-aged, and to teenage me, middle-aged people were basically ancient beings devoted to way too early mornings and way too early bedtimes.

The three of us stepped onto the path. It was lit by a series of tall lights lining the left side, but a few of them were flickering or had already burned out completely.

Thankfully, the full moon helped keep the shadows at bay, and I didn't feel so scared. I also had company. That always helped.

Becca was in the lead. "Kinda creepy out here," she said.

"Perfect," I said.

"Entirely debatable," Ali whispered. "I am not a fan of the dark."

"Well, you picked the wrong short film to help out with," I said. "But I'm glad you're here, man."

Ali and I fist-bumped as Becca slowed, turning and shuffling sideways. "Hey John, I finished reading the script last night."

"Uh-oh."

"No, no, it's good. Great, even. But I have a question about the ending."

"Yeah?" I said.

"Why does Jamie Cameron have to die? She's the main character, dude."

"That's the twist. The thing no one will see coming."

"Feels cheap."

"I am afraid I have to agree with her," Ali said. "I believe the term is 'cop-out.' The audience will be nothing but angered that such a strong character has all of her growth and development ripped away from her in the end."

"Geesh, I wasn't expecting to get grilled tonight. Fourth of July isn't for a few weeks."

Becca snorted. "Lame."

"Yeah, but I got a chuckle."

"Barely," Becca said as she flashed me a smile. "But yeah, cop-out. That's exactly what the ending feels like to me."

"Is your intention to shock the audience?" Ali asked.

We were coming up around a bend now, where three consecutive light poles had burned out. The clearing I wanted to get some footage in wasn't much farther.

"I guess," I said. "I just wanted my film to stand out. I wanted it to be memorable."

"With me as your lead actress, you don't have to worry about that, Johnny Boy." Becca patted me on the cheek.

"Fine, I'll change it. Jamie can live."

But I mean, at that point Becca probably could've talked me into anything.

"Up here," I said, motioning to the clearing. "Becca, you'll just run out from the trees, all dirty and scratched. Ali, get started on her makeup."

"Yes, sir," Ali said.

"Wonderful," Becca mumbled.

I stepped off the path and into the clearing. The collection of trees were anything but inviting. At night they usually weren't, but thoughts of my brother's disappearance and death constantly poked at the back of my mind.

These thoughts were out front now.

"It is kind of peaceful," Ali said. He was on one knee and rummaging through the bag of supplies we'd brought. "It is all about how you view it, I suppose. Is this a dark and scary forest? Or is it only a peaceful place to think?"

"Yeah, man, I'm gonna go with it's a dark and scary forest," Becca said, walking past us. She stood tall and brave, though. Not many things seemed to scare her.

I began setting up the camera on the tripod I'd borrowed from school.

"All you have to do is listen," Ali said. We stayed quiet for a few breaths. Then Ali said, "Do you hear it? There is nothing. No birds or animals or insects, not the wind or the traffic. I only hear the beating of my heart. That is peace."

"You're a poet, Ali," I said, smirking. "But I think we aren't hearing anything because it's late and this town isn't exactly party central. People tuck themselves in at eight, Saturday or not."

"Sounds like Ohio in a nutshell," Becca said. She had started smearing her arms with the fake blood from Party City.

"You know, John, you too can be poetic," Ali said, "if only you cursed less."

"Duly noted, ass-clown." I raised my eyebrows at him. "Hey, guess where I learned that one from…"

"Touché," he said.

"You guys are cute," Becca teased. Her arms were now slathered red. She glowered down at Ali. "Hey, watch it!"

"Sorry," Ali said, pulling a pair of scissors away from her clothing. He was snagging and cutting holes in the cotton of Becca's shirt.

"So anyway," I said, ignoring them, "here's the first shot I want." I made a rectangle with the thumb and index finger of each hand and framed the path of fallen leaves in front of me. "I think this is called a tracking shot—"

"I thought you were a cinephile," Becca said.

"Eh, I just watch the movies. I don't know the terms."

"Perhaps you should read a book," Ali offered. "That is, if you know how to read."

"Oooh, burn!" Becca promptly high-fived Ali, who was all smiles.

"I'll give ya that one," I said. "But c'mon, let's focus here. I'm gonna start low and gradually raise the camera up to the branches and the moon behind." I gave them a short example.

"Eerie," Becca said. "I like it."

"Hopefully I can get it on the first try, but it's kinda cold out here and I'm shaking. If I nail this one, then I'm gonna get some more shots of the trees for the transition sequences. You following?"

To be fair, I wasn't sure I was following myself, but Ali and Becca nodded.

"Great. Ali, can you do me a favor and go around and smear some of that fake blood on the nearby pale tree trunks, and any big rocks you can find? Be on the lookout for anything that might be creepy. Think *Blair Witch* creepy. You've seen that movie?"

"Unfortunately I have," Ali said. "I understand your meaning, and I will do my best." Ali grabbed the bottle of fake blood and went to work.

"All right. Becca, I'm gonna have you coming out from right there." I pointed at the tree line. "Those two big ones. Burst through like you're running for your—"

"Life, got it," she finished.

I shot her a thumbs-up, and then we got to filming.

For this scene, it turned out that I was a bit of a perfectionist. The first try was not great, so I scrapped it, called for another take, and tried again.

I told myself the third time was the charm, and proceeded to make it even worse. Before I knew it, we were on take twelve and I was starting to get frustrated.

Ali, now done smearing blood and upping the creep factor of the set, stood behind, watching. He hadn't said a word, but I snapped at him. I know, it was wrong. I was just looking for an outlet and I chose him, the poor guy.

"Ali!" I shouted. "Go make yourself useful and scout around some more or something! *Please!*"

He looked at me like I'd slapped him across the face. "Forgive me, I did not mean to—"

"Just go, dude!"

"John, maybe we should call it for the night," Becca said.

"No. We're almost there. C'mon."

She sighed. "Whatever." Then she went back to her place at the tree line.

Ali left us, going up the path. I was already starting to feel guilty, but I buried the feeling and hit record on my camera.

A few takes later, I was ready to give up. I pointed at the ground to the left of Becca. "Can you stumble right there, where that little ditch is? Do that on this run and I think we got—"

From the distance came a terrified scream. I jumped.

Ali. That was Ali.

Becca and I looked at each other, both of our faces as pale as the full moon above.

"Ali?" I shouted.

He didn't answer.

"Dude! Ali!"

We ran toward the path as he screamed again. "John! Becca!"

My heart raced, thumping harder and faster than my sneakers on the brick path.

I stumbled through a deadfall with Becca

behind me, and then around a bunch of skinny trees. About twenty feet ahead, I saw the glow of Ali's flashlight.

"What's going on?" I shouted. "What's wrong?"

"Hurry!"

"Oh my God," Becca was saying. "What is that smell?" Her voice was muffled, like she had covered her nose and mouth. It was about this time I caught a really heinous scent.

It belonged to something I hadn't known yet. It belonged to death.

"What is it?" I said, exploding through the brush where Ali was standing.

"This," Ali said, and he shined his light at the ground. "I...I don't know."

"Holy fuck," Becca gasped.

I took one look at the corpse and doubled over, dry heaving. A ham-and-cheese-sandwich-stomach-acid concoction shot up my throat, but I flexed my abdomen and held it down before I puked everywhere.

After a few seconds, I glanced at the corpse again—or what was left of it.

You know what? I don't know if I can rightfully call it a *corpse*. It was just parts, really.

The only identifying pieces were a hoof, a

snout, and shards of antlers. The rest—the middle—had been ripped open, and most of the innards were gone. What was left here was a mess of glistening red ribs and vertebrae. Even the pelt was shredded. Tufts of blood-stained fur lay around it like stuffing.

"I'm gonna be sick," Becca said and turned around. I heard her vomiting a few feet behind me.

I continued staring at the puddle of death, my brain trying to rationalize what I was looking at. Was it a prank? Maybe some dumb teenagers left it out here to scare people. Only…the deer was far enough off the path that no one would see it on a casual stroll. So what would be the point?

"What happened to it?" Ali asked. His voice was quiet. He sounded defeated. I could tell he was not prepared for something like this.

Man, who could be? I tried telling myself that this was nature. The woods were where the animals lived and the woods were where animals died. But I couldn't mute the alarms going off in the back of my mind.

"It's a deer," I said. "A buck. Something got it. Another animal, I mean." I shook my head. There was no way I sounded convincing.

"The poor thing," Ali said. He closed his eyes,

which gleamed wetly in the moonlight, and whispered a prayer in Arabic.

"C'mon, let's get out of here," I said. "We can't do anything for it now." I sighed and put on a fake smile, trying not to look as terrified as I felt. "You okay, Becca?"

"Peachy," she answered, wiping her lips.

"You coming, Ali?" No answer. "Ali?"

"John," he said. "You did tell me to seek out *creepy* things within the forest, did you not? If this is not *creepy*, I do not know what is." He waved a hand at the mutilated...*thing* beside him.

I grimaced and shook my head. I was thinking about *Apocalypse Now* and *Cannibal Holocaust*, movies from the seventies and the eighties. Both of them were infamous for *actually* killing the animals used on set. Owen had told me about that. Had I not known going into the viewing, I might've liked the films, but because I *did* know, I couldn't ever get behind them. Both films left a bad taste in my mouth.

I said, "No. Let's leave it."

Exploiting this felt wrong.

Ali nodded. "I agree." He mumbled something else in Arabic as we started toward Becca and the path. A few steps in, Ali's hand gripped the back of my shirt.

"What?"

"I heard something. Did you?"

Right then, the only thing I was hearing was the rush of blood roaring in my head. "No," I said. "What was it?"

Something snapped behind us.

My muscles tensed, but some important organ in my stomach quivered and went loose. This wasn't a soft *crack* from a snapping twig. This was like the *crack* of a lightning bolt.

As I turned and looked toward the sound, I found it suddenly difficult to breathe.

"Guys?" Becca said. "What was that?"

"I don't know," I answered. "I think—"

Leaves rustled in the direction of the mutilated deer. Something was coming at us, moving so fast it was almost a blur.

I spun around and watched the distant figure in budding horror. At first, I thought it was a person. It stood and strode on two feet like one. But there was no way. People didn't move like that. It had to be an animal.

But what kind of animal? Fucking *Bigfoot?*

Whatever it was, I could tell it was not friendly.

I tugged on Ali's sleeve. "Dude, we gotta go —*now!*"

"Guys? Guys!" Becca screamed.

Arms flailing, hearts thundering, we scrambled to the path, following Becca's voice. She caught us and we almost all went down in a heap.

A few seconds later, the thing burst through the brush and onto the path. It was lit by a pool of moonlight, standing twenty feet from us. I saw it in all of its horror, and I couldn't believe what I was seeing.

My brain tried to reject it, tried to do more rationalizing. But like the mutilated corpse we had found moments ago, there was no rationalizing this.

From head to toe, the creature was covered in silver fur and sinewy muscle. It stood on two legs, slightly hunched, its arms long enough to brush the brick path. Claws protruded from its slender fingers, also terribly long. Its legs were half-bent like the hind legs of a dog or a wolf.

I thought it had to be the result of some evolutionary hiccup or a lab experiment gone wrong, stuck in a purgatory between man and beast.

I was thinking this until I got a better view of its face, which wasn't anything close to human. It had a long snout and a mouth full of fangs. Bright red blood was matted beneath its lower jaw.

We stared at it as the creature regarded us with crazed eyes redder than the blood around its lips. I believed it was sizing us up, and neither Ali, Becca, or myself were able to move.

A growl rumbled from its chest, building into a full-fledged roar. To this day, I swear the surrounding trees trembled. Then the creature fell over on all fours. The fur on the back of its head and neck raised in hackles as it snarled. Silver saliva dribbled from its fangs. It took a step forward, raised its snout, and sniffed the air.

And then it howled.

Ali gripped my forearm, squeezing so tightly I felt my bones give in. Any harder and they might've snapped, but in that moment there was no pain, only fear.

We were going to die. This thing, this creature, this *abomination*, was going to rip us open and shred our guts like it had done to the buck.

Listen, I would love to tell you I was brave. I would love to tell you how I stepped toward the creature and roared back, but then I wouldn't be telling you the truth.

I didn't do anything besides stand there and

almost piss my pants. There wasn't much I could do. We would never be able to outrun this creature. It would chase us down faster than a starving lion.

Because I knew this, because I had already accepted my fate, I froze.

Thankfully, I was not alone, and thankfully, Ali and Becca felt no guilt or had any qualms about screaming.

They screamed at the top of their functioning lungs, and it was their screams that saved us.

"Help! Help!" Becca said.

"Help!" Ali echoed.

The creature stopped and stood upright, glaring at us with its almost human eyes. Its upper lip rose in a snarl, and it growled again.

I was transfixed by the length and sharpness of its fangs. How easily those teeth could sink into our flesh. How easily they could tear us to pieces.

And then the creature snapped its head to the left, as if it heard something. In my peripheral vision, I saw a flashlight beam cut through the darkness. Footsteps rustled through the leaves.

"Hey! I know you're out here!" a man hollered.

I recognized the voice.

The creature turned its snout upward and

sniffed the air. It huffed, a mist of spittle lit by the full moon.

Something had changed in the creature's eyes. The wild look had transformed into a look I associated with fear or uncertainty—maybe even recognition. Then it fell to all fours and took off back the way it had come as Tim Thompson emerged on the path.

"John?" Mr. Thompson said, his brow wrinkled in confusion. "What the hell are you kids doing out here?"

With his right hand, he slipped something silver into his pants pocket before his flashlight totally blinded me.

I didn't even blink. I couldn't.

What I was able to do was fall to my knees. The adrenaline, the fear, the *relief*—it was all too much, and my body couldn't take it anymore.

The blackness, not of night but of unconsciousness, reached out to me.

And as I drifted away, I remember thinking: *Holy shit, he has a gun… Mr. Thompson has a gun…*

CHAPTER 8
SCHEMES

MY EYES FLUTTERED open in my own living room, and for a few seconds I thought I had been dreaming. Everything had been a horrible nightmare. It wasn't the summer of '09 anymore but the summer of '08, and Owen was still alive. When October came, I wouldn't let him go out with his friends and he would be safe and we would be happy and—

A gentle hand shook me. "John?" Ali whispered.

I didn't meet Ali until after Owen's accident. What had happened wasn't a nightmare. It was real. I groaned. There was a terrible taste in the back of my throat, bitter and metallic like blood.

I was slumped over on the couch. Ali was

leaning over the arm, his trembling fingers resting on my shoulder.

"Are you okay?"

"What do you think?" Becca said behind me. "Are any of us okay? How could we be after...after *that?*"

I inhaled deeply. The world around me was materializing, becoming concrete.

"Let him be for a second, young man," said a third voice. "He's had a shock. He just needs to get his bearings back."

Carefully, I craned my neck to the right and saw Mr. Thompson standing in the front foyer by the open door. No gun bulged from his pocket, but there wasn't a chance I'd imagined that. Was there?

His lips moved, but the words didn't register. I was too focused on examining him. Something was off. He appeared to be the same Mr. Thompson I'd known since we moved to Pickwick, in his striped polo shirt tucked into khaki shorts ending an inch above the knee, a leather braided belt holding them up, white socks high on his shins, but the look in his eyes had changed.

I began to grow suspicious.

"John?" he said, his voice a little more urgent.

"Huh?"

"I asked when your mother will be home. Should I give her a call? Do we need to take you to the hospital? I'll tell ya, all the fake blood this young lady had smeared on her really threw me for a loop!"

"Call his mom?" Becca said. She paced back and forth behind the couch. "I think we need to call the fucking Army or the National Guard."

Mr. Thompson ignored her, but his upper lip lifted in a semi-snarl. I'm guessing because of Becca's explicit language. Mr. Thompson was basically a choir boy.

"What was it?" I said.

It couldn't be what I thought it was. That was impossible.

"I didn't see it, buddy," Mr. Thompson said. "Probably just an animal. The dark has a way of playing tricks on your eyes." He laughed in a condescending way and put his hands on his narrow hips. *Stupid kids,* he was probably thinking. "Maybe Daisy Johnson's poodle got out again. Now I don't know if that merits a call to the military, but at the very least, I'll phone it into animal control in the morning. Could be a rabid dog on the loose."

"We know what we saw," Becca said, a hint of venom in her tone. "And that wasn't a rabid dog—"

"Perhaps it was a bear," Ali said. "It stood on two legs at one point. Bears are known to do that, are they not?"

"Oh boy," Mr. Thompson said. "That there is concerning." He was shaking his head and clucking his tongue. "I better go check on Mary, make sure she doesn't wake up and come out looking for me." He wrinkled his brow, the expression showing concern, but his eyes were empty of it. I thought they seemed a little wild, maybe even nervous. "Are you sure you're all unharmed?"

Becca started to say something, but I cut her off, "Yes, I think we're fine."

"Good. Good. I suggest you three stay indoors until this is sorted. I'll give the sheriff a call as soon as I'm home." Mr. Thompson smiled at us. It lacked warmth. "If you need me, I'm right down the street. Do you have my phone number?"

"Yes, sir," I said. "It's on the fridge." Being gone late most nights, my mother had built an exhaustive list of numbers to call in case of an emergency. I think even 9-1-1 was written on that note, as if we could forget it.

"Wonderful." He opened the door. "Stay inside. Call me if you need me."

As soon he started down the walkway, I got up

on my shaky legs, went and turned the deadbolt, and latched the chain.

"What the fuck is going on?" Becca asked. "Why was he so calm about that?"

"He did not see what we saw," Ali said. "It fled. We are alive thanks to him."

Becca held her hands out. "What even was *it?*"

I looked at them. "Really?"

"What?" Becca said.

"No one's gonna say it?"

"Say what?" Ali asked.

"You all saw the same thing I saw, right?" I shuffled over to the windows and jimmied them to make sure they were locked. Not that a thin pane of glass would stop that thing.

"I mean, it looked like a…" Becca began. "No, that's stupid."

"Stupid?" I said. "No. Crazy? Yeah. Definitely."

"You don't really think…?"

"I do," I said. "I think it was a werewolf."

Besides us actually seeing it—although it had been dark—there were too many coincidences to ignore. The full moon, how it stood on two legs, the almost human-like tone it made when it howled. And most damning of all to me, what had happened to my brother last fall.

I told Ali and Becca all of this as we sat in my living room, as far away from the door and windows as possible.

"And you think Mr. Thompson is...what? The werewolf?" Becca said. She rubbed her face with one hand. "Oh God, I can't believe those words actually came out of my mouth."

I tilted my head. "No. Unless he could be in two places at once, and that's impossible."

"This whole thing is impossible!" Becca said.

"Fair point. Still, no way. The transformation couldn't be that quick and quiet. He would've shown up on the path naked—or at least in ripped clothes. I think the werewolf heard him coming and it got spooked."

"Why wouldn't it just kill and eat us all?"

I shrugged. "Not sure, but Mr. Thompson had a gun. I saw it before I...passed out." Yeah, I wasn't too proud of doing that, but hey, at least I didn't wet myself.

"I did not see a weapon," Ali said.

"Me neither," Becca added.

"Well, I did. I'm sure of it," I said. "So that begs

the question: what the hell is he doing out in the woods that late with a gun?"

"His house is not far from the path," Ali said. "Perhaps he heard the commotion and wanted to help."

Becca said, "I don't know about you guys, but if I hear some crazy shit like that at night, I'm not running into the dark woods to try and help, gun or not. That's borderline insane."

I nodded. "True. And we were pretty deep in. I don't think he would've heard much of anything if he was in his house like we're assuming. No. I think he was already out there. I think he was out there looking for the werewolf."

"Okay, that's *actual* insanity," Becca said.

"He knows something. I don't know what it is, but he does, and I wanna find out."

Becca snorted. "What? Are you serious? We need to get the cops involved."

"Or the Ghostbusters," Ali said.

"It's a werewolf, not some vengeful spirit," I said. Although a werewolf ghost did sound pretty badass.

"Whatever," Ali said. "They are most certainly better equipped to deal with this situation than we are."

"Also true," I agreed. "But…"

Becca stood up. "But it's official, I've left Pickwick and moved to Crazy Town."

"You saw it, Becca," I said.

"That's exactly what I mean," she said. "I'm in Crazy Town *because* I believe it. I *actually* believe it."

To be honest, I was surprised. Of the three of us, Becca was the one most grounded in reality. She should've been laughing all this off and calling us dumb for believing we had seen a supernatural creature in the forest, but she wasn't.

Which got me thinking.

"Have you seen it before?" I asked her.

Becca pulled at the hem of her dirty and fake-blood stained shirt. "What? No. I think I'd know." She paused and studied me. "Okay, yeah, I don't know. There was this one time at work a few months ago. I closed that night, so I was taking the trash out from my register—I hate doing it, especially when it's dark. It's a long-ass walk and there's like one light back there. Then there's Jimmy, this asshole stocker who thinks it's hilarious to hide in the shadows and pop out and scare the living hell out of me, and—"

"Wait, was it a full moon?" I asked.

"Dude, I don't know. That was like six months ago."

"Okay, go on."

"Yeah, so, I was taking the trash out, heading toward the dumpsters, and I heard this rustling nearby. I stopped and looked around. I remember saying something like, 'Ha-ha, Jimmy, very funny,' because I figured he was pranking me or whatever. Jimmy didn't say anything back, though, and the noise had stopped, so I kept on going." She looked down at her nails, then brought her fingers to her mouth and nibbled the end of her index. "I just wanted to be off the clock, you know? The job sucks. Anyway, I walked a little faster, and when I got to the dumpster I smelled something awful. Like worse than your usual garbage smell, which is saying something, because our dumpster's right next to that steakhouse, Prime Cut. They're always throwing God knows what away."

She took a deep breath, steeling herself to go on. Whatever she saw back then had terrified her, I could tell.

"Well, okay, so I got to the dumpster and tossed my two bags in, and that was when I heard something else. It was like this wet *slurping* sound. Almost like chewing." Her voice weakened, wavered. "I had my apron over the bottom half of my face, and I was scared shitless, but curiosity killed the cat and all that. I leaned to get a peek through the slit in the fence that's around the dumpsters, and I saw this…I dunno…this kneeling person. It was eating some of the old meat from the steakhouse, I think. Eating like it hadn't had food in weeks." Becca swallowed and shook her head.

"What did it look like?" I asked.

"It was…it was hairy and naked, but it wasn't a…it wasn't a werewolf."

"Could it have been?"

"I don't know. I wasn't gonna ask it for a picture, you know? I took off. I mean, I was too scared to even scream."

"Perhaps it was a…a…what's the word? A homo?" Ali said.

"What does their sexual orientation matter?" Becca asked, confused.

"He means *hobo*," I said.

"Ah, yes. That is what I meant."

"Pickwick's too uptight for a homeless person to hang around," Becca said. "Cops would kick them out in a heartbeat."

"You can't remember if there was a full moon?" I said.

"It's possible." She shrugged. "It was cloudy all day, though. I remember that."

"It has to be the same creature," I said. "You just saw it before it was fully transformed. Maybe the overcast moon slows the process down or something, I dunno."

"I really think we should just call the cops," Becca said.

"No way." I stood up and grabbed a picture of Owen off the mantle. His eighth grade portrait. "The same cops said my brother died by misadventure and that wild animals ate his body. More I think about it, the more I think they don't know what they're doing."

The others avoided my eye contact.

"This is proof that explanation was bullshit. I think this thing killed Owen…and I'm going to stop it before it kills anyone else."

What followed my words was silence.

Ali shifted uncomfortably in his chair. Then Becca said, "How the hell do you suppose you're gonna do that?"

"I don't know. I'll figure out a way. We can't let it keep killing."

"You're crazy," Becca said.

"Maybe, but this is my fight and my fight alone."

Ali turned his eyes up at me now and put his hand out in front of him. "No, John, you are not alone. I will help you avenge your brother."

I smiled at him, putting my hand on top of his. What would I do without this guy?

Becca said, "What are you, the Power Rangers or something?"

Ali was looking at her expectantly.

"You guys don't have to do this," I said. "It's going to be dangerous."

"I know we do not," Ali said, still waiting on Becca.

"Really—" I said.

Becca sighed loudly. "Fine, damn it. I'll help you, but only because we'll probably get famous for killing a werewolf." She put her hand over ours.

Yeah, I guess we did kind of look like the Power Rangers.

Becca left some time around one, but Ali stayed the night, not wanting to walk home alone in the dark. I didn't blame him.

We did no more work on the film, and we certainly kept the topics of conversation off of the werewolf. Instead, we played a board game.

The only one I had all the pieces to was *Candy Land*, and it got intense. We got so into it that Ali almost flipped the table when he got stuck on a Licorice Space near the end. He was pretty competitive, actually.

Still, it was great. It got our minds off the horror we had witnessed earlier.

Ali had left at first light. A werewolf, he said, was truly scary, but his father's wrath after finding he had stayed out all night would be worse. I had watched him make his way down the street and around the corner.

I waited until the blinds in his own upstairs bedroom, which I could see from my house, opened and closed three quick times. That was the signal that he was in the clear. Nothing had gotten him, but most importantly, his father hadn't either. Beyond tired, I crawled back into bed and fell asleep almost instantly.

I woke sometime around eleven, the bright sun streaming through my curtains. In the broad daylight, I didn't feel so scared anymore. I also didn't feel like any of it had happened. It seemed distant and foggy, like a bad dream fading away.

I went downstairs and inhaled a bowl of cereal. My mother was in the living room, sitting on the couch. The TV was playing some local news program.

A man in Gelton, a few towns over, was talking about how all his cattle were slain in the night. My stomach soured, and the reality of the night before crashed into me like a derailed train. The man said he had no idea what had done it. He went the same route as Mr. Thompson had—wild animals.

I shook my head and went into the bathroom, where I splashed some cold water on my face and brushed my teeth. After putting on a fresh change of clothes, I headed for the door.

"Hi, Mom! Bye, Mom!" I said as I leaned over the back of the couch and kissed her cheek.

"Where are you off to in such a hurry?"

"Ali and I are going to the park. Some guys from school wanted to play pickup basketball, and they needed a ninth and tenth for full court. I wanted to get some warm-up shots in before the games start—"

"Basketball, John? When's the last time you even touched a ball?"

"Well, I peed first thing when I got up—"

"Ah-ah! I don't want to hear that disgusting talk. I get enough of that at work."

"Sorry. But you did say I needed to get out more, and that summer's wasted indoors and all that. I'm not crazy about basketball, but Ali loves it."

"Him? Crazy about basketball? But he's so short…"

I shrugged. "Dynamite comes in small packages."

My mother nodded, eying me warily. "Well, at what park?"

"Sunny. Right down the road."

Her wary eyes brightened and she relaxed. I knew she'd be okay with that. Sunny Park was only a few blocks away. Where I was really going was a little farther than that, but I figured she'd buy me playing sports over me willingly taking a trip to the town library, even after my reading binge a few months ago.

"Just be careful." She checked her wristwatch. "And at least be home for dinner, okay? Stir fry tonight."

"Sounds delicious. I'll be here." I kissed her

again on the cheek, told her I loved her, and then I left.

The head librarian at the Pickwick Branch Library was a pleasant old woman named Mrs. Corn.

She was almost stereotypical in her appearance. She wore a classic white cardigan over a high-necked gray blouse buttoned all the way up in spite of the June heat, and a long skirt that matched the color and plainness of her blouse.

Her short hair was fluffy and white. Big cat-style glasses hung around her neck on a chain. She looked like she'd smack you with a ruler if you made more noise than a soft whisper.

Fittingly enough, given her occupation, you couldn't judge this particular book by her cover. Mrs. Corn never shushed anyone, and she was always helpful and sweet, even when others weren't.

She recognized me as soon as I walked in, calling me by name and asking how my mother was doing, even though I've maybe met her twice and hadn't been to the library in ten months.

If my mother hadn't been an all-star around the

library and the local secondhand book store, I believe Mrs. Corn still would've remembered me.

"My mom's doing good. Much better, yeah."

"That is wonderful to hear, John! Do tell her we miss her dearly at the book club. I hope she returns soon."

"I'm sure she will, but I'll tell her."

Mrs. Corn smiled. It was a very grandmotherly smile that made me think of cheek pinches, homemade chocolate chip cookies, and powdery-scented perfume.

"Now, may I help you find anything today?"

"I think I'm just browsing," I said. "Thank you."

"Enjoy, dear. I'll be at the circulation desk if you need me."

I flashed Mrs. Corn a smile back and then went toward the rows and rows of books. It only took going down one aisle before I got confused and went back for help.

"Uh, excuse me, Mrs. Corn. I guess I could use a little assistance," I said.

"Of course, dear. What are we in the mood for today? Something fun and adventurous? We have quite a selection of Edgar Rice Burroughs. He is responsible for the timeless characters of Tarzan and John Carter. I'm quite sure you've heard of those two famous characters, no?"

I nodded.

"Or perhaps you would like something else? How about a classic to get a head start on your summer reading?" Mrs. Corn motioned to a display near the Teen/YA section. "I believe incoming juniors are required to read *Frankenstein* by Mary Shelley."

"Actually, I just read that one a couple months back."

Another lie.

"Wonderful!" Mrs. Corn beamed like I had told her she picked the winning numbers in the Mega Millions. "I would expect nothing less from Dolores Carver's son. So then, what sounds good to you, young man?"

I cleared my throat and focused on the pen chained to the circulation desk instead of Mrs. Corn's smiling face. "I'm looking for something about…" I lowered my voice and leaned forward a bit. "*Werewolves.*"

Mrs. Corn let out an exaggerated gasp. "Ooh, a horror lover, are we? Well, we do have an extensive collection of Stephen King. I am not too familiar with his work, but I am sure he has written a werewolf book over the course of his long career. If not, I can make other, more *dated* suggestions. Although their prose may read a bit stiffly, I assure you they are classics." She pushed her glasses up her nose, and, leaning so close to her computer screen she could've kissed it, she began typing slowly with the index fingers of each hand.

"Well…no, I was thinking more like something real."

Mrs. Corn stopped poking the keys. "*Real?*"

"Yeah, something about *real* werewolves."

A moment of silence followed as Mrs. Corn studied my face. When she realized I wasn't joking, she laced her fingers together and rested her hands in front of her. "John, werewolves aren't real, dear."

I chuckled, albeit a bit uncomfortably. "Yeah, I know, but I want something that reads like it's real. Like a serious kinda account on them, their history, their strengths, their weaknesses… I don't know what you'd call it, but I know there's probably a million books on Bigfoot and the Loch Ness monster, and no one can *actually* prove they're real either."

"Ah." Mrs. Corn nodded. "I see. What you are referring to is called *Cryptozoology*."

"I don't know that word."

"It is the study of animals—or *creatures*—whose existence isn't necessarily proven. Bigfoot, the Loch Ness monster, *werewolves*, and more."

I nodded, snapped my fingers, and rapped my knuckles on the desk. "Bingo."

Mrs. Corn smiled that warm grandmotherly smile again, and then she began tapping away at her keyboard. A little faster this time, as if my enthusiasm had renewed her own.

"Hmm, let's see," she said, squinting at the screen and mumbling to herself a couple of times. "Ah, yes, right here. We have three titles that may be of interest to you: *A Guide to Hypertrichosis* by Theodore Fuller, *The Lycanthropy Curse* by S. F. Huckland, and lastly, *Phases of the Moon and Lunacy* by one Georgia Zachary. None have been checked out in...let's see"—she moved her finger across the results and whistled—"my, oh my. Not for many years."

"Not surprised. It doesn't seem like a popular subject," I said.

"I do see others in the county system. I could order them for you. It will take two to three business days. Would that be something you'd like?"

"These three are good for now, thank you."

"Wonderful." Mrs. Corn wrote the titles down

on a sticky note. She caught the attention of one of the librarian's assistants, a college-aged woman in more modern attire of capris pants and a yellow City of Pickwick *Reading Bonanza* t-shirt, and said, "Miss Robin, would you please locate these titles for Mr. Carver here?"

Miss Robin smiled, nodded, and dove into the stacks. While we waited, Mrs. Corn said, "I know it's none of my business, but you aren't having werewolf troubles, are you?" The gleam in her eye matched the playful smirk on her face.

I chuckled. "No. Just research."

"That is a wonderful word, isn't it?" Mrs. Corn said. "May I ask what for?"

I didn't have an answer prepared. I guess I probably should've. Mrs. Corn was as curious as she wanted the library-goers to be.

Hesitating for only a moment, I told Mrs. Corn about the film festival and the short movie I was making for it. I told her I had the whole plot figured out except for the ending.

The good guys were facing off against the big bad creature, but being how the big bad creature was a supernatural entity, you couldn't exactly call the cops on it and have it arrested.

"Inspiration," Mrs. Corn said, nodding. "I see.

Well, John, you've come to the right place. Our shelves are lined with only the finest inspiration!"

Miss Robin's flat heels clicked across the floor. I looked over my shoulder and saw her smiling at us, the books clutched to her chest. She set them on the counter, and Mrs. Corn scanned their barcode stickers. Then a few keystrokes later, a receipt rolled out of the printer.

Mrs. Corn opened the first book, *A Guide to Hypertrichosis*, which had no cover art and looked like it was written maybe two hundred years ago. She laid the slip on the title page, closed it so it stuck out like a bookmark, and said, "These are all due two weeks from now, but if you would like to renew them, you needn't come in. Just give us a call and we'll extend the due date by another seven days, unless more than five others are on the waiting list." She leaned forward and whispered, "I do, however, doubt anyone will be clamoring for these."

I glanced at the stack of books. They looked about as uninteresting as they sounded. If you didn't know the subject matter, you'd probably think they were the kind of books you'd find in some ancient college professor's study, full of terms you've never heard or knew the meaning of.

"Thank you so much," I said.

"Of course!" Mrs. Corn said. "I look forward to seeing you again, John. Give your mother our best, and good luck on your film submission! I'll be rooting for you!"

I smiled. Her kindness touched my heart. "Thank you, Mrs. Corn. I'll be sure to give you a shout-out in the credits."

She clapped her hands together. "Oh, I can't wait! Hollywood, here I come!"

The day had warmed considerably, and the sun burned bright directly overhead.

As I rode my bike down the sidewalk of Center, the afternoon traffic starting to back up from the lunchtime rush, I wondered again if I really had come a few feet away from an *actual* werewolf.

I laughed to myself. If only Mrs. Corn knew the truth.

I turned into the Sunny Park parking lot. It was deserted at this time except for a few dog walkers and joggers.

The three full-sized basketball courts were also peppered with people shooting around and playing casual games.

The groups of teens and dudes in their twenties who played full court five-on-five wouldn't be there for a few hours at least.

Once the heat broke, there would be dozens of people on every court, most of them waiting for their turn to play the winners.

I knew this because Owen frequented this park, sometimes playing from morning to sundown. He'd never have to wait either. Winners stayed, and winning was all he seemed to do.

Beneath a black oak tree sat a bench between the baseball field and the courts. It was empty. I rolled my bike through the wavering grass and set it next to the bench. There, in the shade of the wide leaves, I plunked down and cracked open my library books.

What I read seemed like a bunch of nonsense. *A Guide to Hypertrichosis* was basically about people with too much body hair, how to maintain it, how to slow the growth, blah-blah-blah.

While I sympathized with hairy people, this wasn't exactly what I was looking for. It was too scientific. Too *real*.

Sighing, I tossed the book aside and opened *Phases of the Moon and Lunacy*. After about two minutes, I knew *Phases* suffered from a different problem. While not completely scientific, its pages were full of accounts of people who had lost their marbles during the full moon. People going on killing sprees, howling at the night sky, and committing all these depraved acts, only to experience amnesia the next morning. If there was ever a movie adaptation of this book, the tagline on the poster would say *The moon made them do it.*

So, despite it not being what I needed, I read on for a while because it was entertaining. Maybe an hour passed before I looked up.

The park had gotten a little busier. One of the distant pavilions was choked with people of all ages. The smell of grilling burgers and hot dogs drifted on the air, and my stomach grumbled. I ignored the hunger and opened *The Lycanthropy Curse* without much hope.

Curse opened with terms I couldn't pronounce, and each page was a wall of microscopic print—so not really a hot start. At least *Phases of the Moon and Lunacy* had the occasional picture to break up the words.

I flipped to the table of contents, found a chapter called "Cures and Remedies," and began skimming it.

I was about ready to call it quits when my eyes

stumbled over a passage about rabies. The theory the author proposed was this: if you could find a cure for rabies, you could find a non-lethal cure for lycanthropy.

I scratched my head. A rabies vaccine already existed, didn't it? Then it hit me. This book wasn't old—it must've been *ancient*. It definitely looked like it.

I laid my pencil (can't highlight public property and all that) in the middle crease and turned to the copyright page, bringing it about two inches from my eyes.

The book was copyrighted in the year 1867 by an English publisher I had never heard of. The author, a person named S. F. Huckland, must've died before the rabies vaccine was made public.

Either that or Huckland had written a sequel that wasn't in the county library system. I'd have to do more research about it when I got home, which would be a pain with how slow our internet usually—

"He's not going to hurt you," a man's voice suddenly said. "But he's gonna act like he will. Don't scream for help, it'll only make it worse."

It sounded so close, I jumped and the book fell onto the grass at my feet with a muffled thump.

"What the hell?"

"Remain calm," the voice said. "The Hunter's almost there, kid."

I stood and peered around the oak. There was fifty yards of open grass between me and the woods that separated the park from the road to the north, but I saw no one, and I knew the man couldn't be in the trees.

He had seemed only a few feet away from my ears—almost as if he had spoken in my head.

Oddly, the voice was familiar. Like its location, though, I couldn't pinpoint it.

My best course of action was to flee. Get closer to people before I found myself in the kind of trouble I couldn't run from.

But it was too late.

When I turned to gather my books, a man I had never seen before was there waiting for me.

He stood the way Clint Eastwood did in the old Sergio Leone Spaghetti Western films before a gunfight, but that was as far as the resemblance to the actor went.

This man was haggard and gray, his face full of scars and wrinkles. He wore a dark jacket and pants made from some heavy material too hot for summer. And like his face, his clothing was marred in places.

He smelled of fire, smoke, and sweat.

This man was not the owner of the first voice that had warned me. I stared at him for a long moment, thinking he had to be on drugs or that he was a homeless person passing through Pickwick, and I just happened to pick the wrong bench to sit on this afternoon.

"Stay out of my way, kid," the man grumbled.

"W-what?" I mumbled.

"I said, stay the hell out of my way."

I stepped to the side.

The man didn't move. He spat on the ground, allowing me a flash of his yellowed teeth. "A smart-ass too, huh?"

I couldn't decide if the man was in his fifties or his *one-hundred-and-fifties.*

"You know what I'm talking about. It's *mine*. All you and your little friends are gonna do is get in my way and get killed. Go hide under your blankie and pray it don't pick up your scent."

My initial confusion changed to fear, and this fear started in my heart. As I realized what the man had referenced, it began to branch in various directions across my body.

"The w-wolf?" I managed.

"*The w-wolf?*" he mocked and spat again. "Call it that again and I'll rip your throat out myself. 'Cause it ain't no wolf." He smiled, but it never touched his dark eyes. "See? It's this kinda ignorance that gets dummies like you torn up."

"It's a monster," I said. "I saw it last night."

"I know you did. You and that skinny man fucked it all up. And you don't wanna know what happens to you if you do it again."

He took a step forward, the wind catching his jacket and revealing the biggest revolver I have ever laid eyes on holstered to his belt. He rested his left hand on the butt of the weapon, and I saw on the back of his hand there was a faded tattoo of a crossing, curled tentacles.

I lost my balance and sat on the bench hard enough to bite my tongue.

"*Stay out of my way,*" he said.

The man turned right, heading around the big oak tree and toward the woods at my back. By the time I was able to get to my feet—only a few seconds after I'd fallen—he was gone, vanished like smoke in the wind.

I rushed home, looking over my shoulder constantly.

My mother was rummaging through the refrigerator for the stir fry ingredients.

"Back already?" she called.

"Yeah."

"Did you win?"

"Huh?"

"The basketball games. Did you win any?"

"Oh," I shouted from the hall. "Yeah, a couple. I'm not too good, but Ali is a wizard."

More lies.

"Wonderful! Dinner'll be ready in a few."

"I'm gonna wash up, and then I'll be down." I started up the stairs and stopped halfway. "Hey, Mom!"

"Yes, honey?"

"Mind if Ali comes over to eat?"

"Of course not! That boy is always welcome."

"Thanks!"

I changed my clothes and went straight to the phone. I told Ali he had to come over as soon as possible.

"Why?" he asked. "John, are you hurt? You sound very frightened."

"I'm okay. I'll tell you more when you get here."

"Listen, John, I am in trouble," he said. "My father knows how late I stayed at your house." He paused. "But then again, he and my brother are not home…"

"Great! Just get your ass over here!"

I hung up, and he was at the front door five minutes later.

"Someone else knows," I said once Ali had greeted my mother and we were in the relative privacy of my bedroom.

"What?"

"About the werewolf, and I'm not talking about Mr. Thompson."

Ali cocked his head. "I do not follow. A secret like this would be difficult to keep."

I told him what had happened earlier at the park. I left out the part about the voice I had heard in my head prior to the stranger's arrival, because that was *too* crazy to admit.

"And do you think he was friendly?" Ali asked about the man.

"He sure as hell wasn't friendly. He threatened to kill me, dude. He said we messed it up for him."

"Is he the werewolf?"

"I don't know… It's possible. Or maybe he's like the werewolf's familiar or something?"

Ali squinted. "Familiar? As in family?"

"No, I mean like Renfield in *Dracula*. You know, like a servant."

"Even I know Dracula is a vampire. What we saw last night was not a vampire."

"True, but just because it's in the movies, doesn't mean it's not real," I said.

"Well, what do we do, then?" Ali was pacing nervously by my bed. He put both hands behind his head and exhaled. "Perhaps we *should* contact the proper authorities…"

I didn't reply.

Honestly, the strange man in the park had rattled me. Our encounter led me to believe that there was more to this than just a case of supernatural creature terrorizes a small town. But what if we were somehow cracking some kind of conspiracy? What if they came after my mother next?

I shook my head. "No. This is still our fight. We'll just have to be a little more careful."

"Dinner's ready!" my mother called from the bottom of the stairs.

"Coming!" I shouted back and then looked at

Ali, whose new fear had brought tears to his eyes. "We're okay for now, I think. There's only, what, a full moon once a month? We'll be better prepared the next time it comes around."

"We will?"

I nodded. "For now, let's be normal teenagers and enjoy summer."

But I was thinking: *How the hell do we do that?*

We ate dinner, but we did not act normal. My mother noticed.

She nodded at Ali. "Everything okay, buddy? You look like you've seen a ghost."

He choked on his water, but I laughed and said, "No, he's just down about losing to me in *Halo*."

"Dumb game," Ali grumbled not so convincingly.

"Exactly!" my mother agreed, holding an open palm out at Ali. "Thank you!"

We finished up, helped do the dishes, and then left to go to Ali's house. His father and brother were helping his newest family members get settled in their house an hour away near Lake Erie and most likely wouldn't be back until the morning. Much to his annoyance, this left his place the perfect spot for us to work on *Creature*.

It reminded me of one of those model homes you can walk through whenever they're building a new housing development. The bare walls were painted a pristine white, the floor was laminate made to look like hardwood, and even the picture frames on the mantle in the living room still had the stock photos inside of them.

I picked one of these frames up and examined it. A mother was cradling a baby, both of them smiling and staring into each other's eyes. Both of them very Caucasian.

"I definitely see the resemblance," I said.

"Pardon?"

I showed him the picture, and he smiled in an almost embarrassed way. "No…it's my father. He is not one for interior decoration. He is waiting for my mother to move here. I think out of fear more than anything else."

"This place could use a woman's touch," Becca said from behind the screen in the living room window.

Ali yelped.

I started a bit but recognized the voice. Unlike

the others that had been scaring me of late, this one was welcome.

"Whoa, when did you get here? I didn't even hear your car," I said, opening the door.

She smiled as she stepped in, a canvas tote bag dangling from her shoulder. I thought her eyes looked funny. Like she had been crying.

"Everything okay?" I asked.

"Yeah...I'm good. It's just, you know, boy troubles."

I wondered if she was talking about Ryan Kensington, almost asked, but decided it was best not to. It was none of my business.

"John knows all about boy troubles," Ali said.

Becca laughed, and I told him that was a good one, but Ali was studying us with a confused expression on his face.

"Oh, that wasn't a joke," I said.

"No, I was talking about your run-in at the park."

"Ooh," Becca set her bag down on the chair near the picture window. "Hot date?"

"No. It was just—"

"Oh hey," she said, parting the curtains (which had a pattern I found eerily similar to a Christmas fruitcake) and pressing her forehead to the glass.

"Isn't that the Thompsons? For a guy who knows about a werewolf, he seems pretty damn relaxed."

I leaned around Ali and saw two figures walking up the street toward the park. Mr. and Mrs. Thompson were talking and holding hands.

"Yeah, that's them," I said.

"His wife is pretty," Becca said. "I love her hair. It's so full and bouncy."

"Yeah," I agreed emptily.

When the Thompsons were farther down the road, I went toward the door and cracked it open.

"John?" Ali said. "Where are you going?"

"I-I don't know," I said. "I think maybe to commit a felony."

"What?" Ali and Becca both said.

"They're not home. C'mon."

"You mean, you want to break into their house?" Becca asked.

"That is a horrendous idea!" Ali said, but I was on the front porch, watching the Thompsons as their silhouettes grew smaller and smaller.

I turned. Becca and Ali were both behind the glass of the storm door, voices slightly muffled. "If he knows something about the werewolf, there's gotta be evidence there, right?"

"You are insane, John!" Ali said.

"Yeah, I'm not disagreeing with you there," I said. "But I don't want to *break in*. I just want to look around. I do have a point, though, don't I?"

"Point or not, what you are talking about can land us in prison! And if the cops are called, I am sure you can guess who they will put in handcuffs first. Yes, the boy from *Terrorist-istan!*"

"We won't get caught, I promise."

"What happened to our plan of acting like normal teenagers?"

"Hey," Becca said, pushing past Ali. "Don't you know that normal teenagers are dumb? This is exactly what a normal teenager *would* do."

"Another good point," I said. "So you're down?"

"If it'll get this werewolf stuff out of your head, sure," Becca said. "The faster we do that, the faster we can film this movie." She tapped her lower lip. "Wait a second...am I the director or are you, John?"

I raised my eyebrows. "What, you don't believe now?"

"I saw...*something.* It was dark and I was afraid. But a *werewolf...?* It's silly, isn't it?"

"Okay," I said, "sure. But I know what I saw." I faced Ali. "Are you down or not, dude?"

He crossed his arms, shook his head. "No. No way. Never."

"Fair enough." To Becca: "And you're down?"

"Why not? I guess I'm feeling a little dangerous today." She cupped my chin, and my body rippled with excitement. "I like this version of John Carver." She let go of me and headed for the sidewalk.

I didn't blame her for not being sold on the werewolf idea. So much of my life during and after this time belonged to the realm of nightmares.

Even as I recount this tale now, I still find myself in disbelief.

I nodded at Ali. "You know what they say, buddy. Nice guys finish last."

His mouth twisted as he weighed his options. Go to jail or impress a girl. Those are tough choices.

"Fine," he finally replied. He had chosen the girl.

Yeah.

Whether we wanted to be or not, we were definitely normal teenagers.

CHAPTER 9
THE HOUSE

"HOW WILL we know if no one's home?" Ali was saying as we went up the sidewalk toward the modest-sized ranch-style house and stopped in front of it. We had to have looked suspicious as hell standing there.

"We just saw him and his wife going up the street," I said.

"What about children? A dog? A security system?" Ali asked.

"No kids, no dog, and dude, c'mon, no one in Pickwick has a security system."

"Someone with something to hide might," Becca said.

I scowled at her, mostly because that was a good point. She was full of those.

"See!?" Ali said. "This is a bad idea."

"Yes. We established that," I said.

"And now we are going to establish if this werewolf shit is real or not. I see no problem with that," Becca said.

"You see no problem with breaking the law?" Ali said. "My friends have lost their minds!"

"When it comes to helping rid the town of werewolves," Becca said, "I guess not." She winked at me.

"Try explaining that to the police," Ali said.

Yeah, that wouldn't go well, I supposed.

Worried myself, I turned to Becca, ready to tell her to forget it, that we could investigate another time, but she was already gone, framed by the immaculately trimmed hedges as she waled up the pathway leading to the front door.

"Becca! Wait!"

She ignored me and kept on going. I will say this: I envied her. The way she walked around like she owned the place, having all that confidence, it was surreal—and it reminded me of my brother in a way.

Me? Well, I overthought every little interaction. *What if there's something in my teeth I didn't notice? No one's going to take me seriously, I'm only a teenager.* That sort of thing.

Becca mounted the brick steps, leaned forward, and rang the doorbell twice. I could hear it from where we were standing on the sidewalk. *Ding-ding, ding-ding.* Then she backed up and clasped her hands behind her back, waiting for someone to answer.

"Double-checking," she said to us.

She turned around and smiled. It was the kind of smile you'd expect her to flash at a customer who was giving her a hard time at the hardware store.

She was bold, I'll give her that.

I scanned around for any onlookers, but the neighborhood was quiet for a summer evening. Everyone seemed to have already gotten their fill of the hot weather.

In Ohio, during the first few days of sunshine, you can barely get down the sidewalk without bumping elbows with someone walking their dog or going for a jog. Parks are packed, ice cream shops have lines that rival the roller coasters at Cedar Point, and the local root beer stand's parking lot is almost always filled.

Not that day, though.

In the distance, all I spotted were a couple of

power-walkers and another family pulling around a red wagon with a little boy sitting in it. Other than them, there were no immediate prying eyes. That's not to say there weren't people peeking through their blinds or behind their curtains.

The faster we got this over with, the better.

Becca said, "Yeah, I'm pretty sure no one's home."

"You cannot be completely sure—" Ali started to say, but Becca hopped off the front porch into the grass, went to the bay window, and peered in.

"Relax, man," she said to him.

"Oh no," he moaned.

"See anything?" I called.

She showed us a thumbs down as she went around the right side of the house. A few seconds later, she said, "Hey! Come here! It's open!"

An unseen force clenched my insides. We were really doing this, and what we were doing was stupid, dangerous, ridiculous, et cetera, but if I stood around and didn't do anything at all, I knew I would've regretted it.

"Can you whistle?" I asked Ali.

"Whistle?"

"Yes."

"Quite loudly, actually." He stuck two fingers in his mouth and took in a deep breath. I stopped him.

"Okay, I believe you. You'll be our lookout. You see the Thompsons, you whistle your heart out, got it?"

"John...this is not a good idea, really—"

"Matter of fact, you see *anyone* coming to snoop around, just whistle. Okay?"

He nodded, his face defeated.

I put a hand on his shoulder. "But you know, like, lay low a bit. Don't make it *obvious* you're being a lookout."

"Not obvious. Understood."

I ran to the side of the house where Becca was waiting at a window, and I took a second to glance over my shoulder at Ali. He was striding back and forth on the sidewalk and humming to himself, looking about as obvious as possible.

I shook my head. No sense in trying there, we'd have to make this quick.

Becca had a side window open about six inches. It was seven or eight feet above the ground, already narrow to begin with. Thin and gangly as I was, I didn't see myself fitting through it.

The nerves were starting to get to me. That, and I heard that shady guy from the park in my head telling me to stay out of his way again, seeing his tattooed hand resting on the butt of his giant revolver in my mind's eye.

I swallowed down my fear as best as I could and said, "We don't have to do this, you know...if you don't want to?"

"Hey, you wanna know for sure, don't you?" She cupped her chin and cracked her neck by turning her head first to the right, then to the left. "Give me a boost."

"You're seriously doing this?"

Man, I was starting to sound like Ali.

"Oh c'mon, John. Quit the choir boy routine. *Yes.* I'm going in there. Then, because your head is too big to fit through the window, I'm gonna unlock the back door and you're coming in with me. Now help me!"

With a firm hand, she gripped my shoulder and forced me down to one knee. She stepped onto my thigh and grabbed the edge of the window. Wobbling, her backside about five inches from my face (and me trying not to pay attention to it), she stretched and opened the window another foot with a grunt of victory.

"Higher," she said.

I got her up higher with relative ease. She climbed inside and landed without making a sound.

A few seconds later, her face was floating in the open window above, smiling, beautiful as ever. She spoke into her wrist like a secret agent in a spy film, but her dialogue leaned more sci-fi.

She said, "Houston, we have landed. So far, no signs of life. The coast is clear." Then she disappeared for a heartbeat before the backdoor groaned open and she motioned me inside.

I was hesitant at first. I mean, Ali wasn't wrong: we were talking about breaking the law here.

But all I had to do was think about Owen, about what had happened to him, about what *could* happen to someone else's brother or son or sister or daughter, and how I could help prevent it by doing this, and the fear went away.

The backdoor gave way to the kitchen. It was small relative to the house. A middle island with a bowl of fresh fruit on it, black and white tile on the floor, an electric stove with a sparkling top, and a refrigerator with French doors. No dishes sat in the sink, but there was a lingering smell of meat, like someone had been frying bacon in a skillet not long ago.

A sign hung above the back door. It read: *All Are Welcome*.

I followed Becca into the dining room. Here was a long wooden table and four high-back chairs. To the left of the entrance stood a cabinet full of china plates. There wasn't even a speck of dust on the glass.

"Are you sure they actually live here?" Becca whispered. She had gone on and was in the living room now. There, the furniture looked like it had never been sat in. The large television mounted on the wall still had the protective plastic around its frame. This place was giving Ali's a run for its money in the sterile department.

"Far as I know," I said. "I've never been inside, but I've seen them inside…if that makes sense. I guess they must be neat freaks."

Becca picked up a framed picture off one of the end tables and examined it.

"Don't touch anything!"

She turned to me. "What?"

"*Fingerprints.* You're gonna leave fingerprints all over."

"Boy, you've been watching way too much *CSI*. They'll never know we were here, for one. And for two, even if they somehow figure out someone got in—which they won't—you really think the *Pickwick Police Department* is gonna send a bunch of cops to dust for prints?" She chuckled. "You've seen those guys. They can barely get their flashlights on. No way they'd dust for prints without accidentally ruining the evidence. Probably burn the house down."

She had a point.

"Well…we can't be too careful."

"John, I think that ship sailed a while ago. Like, you know, when we broke in."

"We're criminals now," I said.

She raised a finger. "Only if we get caught. Which we won't…if Ali does his job." She frowned. "Okay, yeah, maybe we'll get caught. So let's make this snappy."

I peeked through the living room curtains. Ali was leaning against a telephone pole, his head constantly snapping left to right, left to right like he was tweaking on drugs. If anyone saw him, we were fucked.

"I think we should just call it—"

"Bingo!" Becca said from a different dark hallway branching off the living room. I took a few steps toward her voice. She was trying to open a door to what I thought was a linen closet, based on its close proximity to the bathroom.

"What is it?"

Instead of answering, Becca grabbed the knob and rattled it for emphasis.

"The door's locked. I get it."

"Yes. But *why* is it locked?"

I shrugged. "I don't know."

"Oh, John, you're so innocent it's almost sweet." She tugged on the doorknob again. "He doesn't want people to see whatever's in there."

"Maybe it's where he keeps his guns," I said. "He had one last night."

Becca sighed. "Maybe. I doubt it."

"What do you think it is?"

"A sex dungeon," she said. "He strikes me as an assless leather chaps kind of guy."

I laughed.

"But I'll tell you what, it ain't werewolf related. I can guarantee that."

"I knew you didn't believe it," I said.

She shrugged. "Can you blame me?"

"So you just came along and broke into this house with me for what reason?"

She mussed my hair. "Let's call it late-stage teenage rebellion." Then she dropped to the floor, pressed her face against the crack beneath the door, and inhaled deeply.

"Okay," I mumbled, "yeah. This is going weirder than I expected."

"Sniff it," she said, eyes turning up to me.

"I'm not sniffing—"

She almost yanked my arm out of its socket as she pulled me down. Next thing I knew, I was on the hall carpet, my nose pressed into the crack at the bottom of the door like a dog looking for its lost owner.

Yeah, this was a strange time in my life, but it was hardly the strangest.

"Do you smell that?" she asked.

I did. It was a moldy smell, a wet smell. It reminded me of a cave.

"It's the basement," I said.

"Yep, not a tiny closet. Not a gun safe."

"Who locks their basement?" I said mostly to myself.

"We have to see what he's keeping down there." Becca left.

I heard her opening drawers in the kitchen. *Clinks* and *tings* as she riffled through a stranger's belongings.

I did the same in the bathroom, unsure of what

I was even looking for, and I did it a lot more carefully.

I found nothing besides toilet paper and over-the-counter medicine. *Normal* stuff. The longer I looked, the more ridiculous this all seemed.

Had we really seen a werewolf? Or had it just been some weird-ass bear? What about the guy in the park? Did I hallucinate that too?

I glanced in the mirror. Not even the tiniest speck of dried toothpaste obscured my reflection, but I had seen better days. That much was true.

Although I wasn't tired, I definitely looked the part. *Had* looked the part since Owen died.

"DayQuil and cotton swabs," I whispered to myself. "What the hell am I doing here?"

That was it. I marched out of the bathroom, ready to leave. Ali was right—this was stupid. There probably wasn't anything but laundry detergent and cobwebs in the basement.

As I turned at the end of the hall to cut through the living room toward the kitchen where Becca was, she pushed past me. I had to double-take at what she was holding in her hand.

"Becca! Whoa! Why do you have a hammer?"

She gave no answer besides raising it above the locked basement doorknob. I lunged forward as she swung downward, grabbing her wrist before she could strike the brass.

"Watch out!" Becca grunted, pulling away.

"What are *you* doing? This is crazy! We've already broken in, and now you're talking about destruction of property? I thought they'd never know we were here."

"Well, Mr. Boy Scout, plans have changed." She shoved me out of the way with a bump of her hip, and I stumbled into the wall.

Unlike Shakira, Becca's hips had lied. They were deadlier than they looked.

"Wait!" I said. "I have a better idea."

"Yeah?"

"Let me get my camera." I went for the back door, but stopped and held my hand out. "Give me the hammer, for insurance."

She smiled at me guiltily. "Fine."

I left out the way I had come in—dropping the hammer in one of the few open kitchen drawers—and grabbed my camera from the bag where Ali was standing by the telephone pole in front of the house.

He sighed with relief. "Are you finished? Oh, thank—"

"Keep on watching," I shouted. "Almost done!"

Back inside, trying to catch my breath, Becca was still by the locked basement, looking at me all confused.

"Okay...gimme your belt," I told her.

"Um...perv alert?"

"What? No! Just give me your belt. Keep your shorts on."

She frowned. "Why can't I just bust it with the hammer? Really?"

"Your belt, please. Trust me."

She took it off, and I looped it around the handle on my camera. She followed me into the bathroom.

Next to the sink was a laundry chute. I opened the tiny door, measured the width of it with my eyes, and nodded. It would fit. Then I wrapped the far end of the belt around my fist, gripping it tightly, and slipped the camera down the chute, lowering it an inch or two at a time.

It scraped and clanked against the metal, sending vibrating *dings* back toward us.

"Wow, clever," Becca said, leaning against the shower door. "I'm impressed."

I chuckled uncomfortably.

It was not every day the prettiest graduating

senior at Pickwick High compliments something you do, you know.

Beads of sweat had started to pop on my forehead. If I dropped the camera, not only would I have busted the most expensive thing I ever owned, but Mr. Thompson would know exactly who had broken into his house. I hadn't swapped out the memory card yet. All the footage I filmed yesterday was still on it. Footage of Ali and Becca and even a few shots of yours truly. If that wasn't ironclad evidence, I didn't know what was.

Suddenly, the clanking stopped, which meant the camera was hovering near the basement ceiling.

"Make sure you rotate it," Becca said. "Get the full view."

"I'm trying," I said. "It's not exactly easy to control a braided leather belt."

"Hey, that belt was expensive. It's from Hollister."

"I think I saw the same one at Target for five bucks."

Becca rolled her eyes. "You sound like my mom."

I worked the belt like the strings of a marionette for about a minute and a half.

"Okay...I think that's good enough. Hopefully nothing blocked the lens."

As I pulled it up, I caught the sound of voices outside, followed by something high-pitched and shrill.

"Did you hear that?" Becca asked. She put a finger in her ear and wiggled it.

"Yeah, it sounded like a—"

"A whistle," Becca finished.

We looked at each other, eyes as wide as twin full moons.

Oh fuck.

CHAPTER 10
ESCAPE

"HURRY UP!" Becca hissed.

"I'm trying! It's stuck!"

The camera was caught on something, either the edge of the chute or some pipes. I wasn't sure, and I couldn't exactly look down and see, but I was making a ton of noise.

The voices continued outside, and another chimed in. It was Ali.

"He's buying us time," I said and then mumbled, "C'mon...c'mon..."

"That or he's spilling his guts. You saw how nervous he was. Faster!"

"No. He wouldn't do that." I shot her a dark look. "And I'm trying!"

There was a loud *clang* as the camera bashed

into metal. I cringed, wondering on some level of my anxiety-filled and frightened brain how badly I'd damaged the most expensive item I owned.

A lull fell over the outdoor conversation. Had Mr. Thompson heard the banging? The walls were thin, but they weren't *that* thin, were they?

I waited half of a second I didn't have, my ears straining for hushed words, my mind willing their lips to move again.

"Jesus Christ, give me it," Becca whisper-yelled. She took the belt in her right hand and pulled. I didn't let go. It was wrapped too tightly around my fist, and she had given me no time to let go.

So now she was pressed against me and, despite the current predicament we were in, my teenage brain was howling like a rabid animal. She smelled like lavender and steam and freshness, and I wondered if she had just showered before she stopped over at Ali's...and then I started picturing her in the shower, all covered in soap suds, her blonde hair wet and stuck to her tanned skin, and—

"John!"

"Huh?" I shook my head, Becca's voice bringing me back to the present "Yeah, hi?"

She was leaning against the wall, her right arm

disappearing into it, as if the house was devouring her. She was reaching down the chute.

"I almost…got…it—" she grunted.

A series of smaller clangs echoed around the bathroom, and then the camera flopped out of the chute like a fish from the dark depths of the ocean.

Wispy silver cobwebs hung from the Velcro on the side handle and dangled around the lens. The red recording light shined brightly in the bathroom's dimness.

Not bothering to untie the belt from it, Becca shoved the camera against my midsection hard enough to knock out what little breath I was holding in my lungs. She snagged my hand and tugged me into the hallway.

The front door was in the living room. As we cut left toward the kitchen and the back door, I saw the Thompsons' dark silhouettes advancing along the walkway through the sheer curtains.

Mr. Thompson stopped and waved at Ali, who was now at the end of the driveway, and hollered, "Remember what I said, okay? You stay safe out there."

"Yes, sir," Ali replied, his voice more muffled than Mr. Thompson's.

My heart thundered in my chest, rattling my

ribcage to the point of pain. I wouldn't have been surprised if I had dropped dead on the spot.

"Nice kid," Mr. Thompson said to his wife.

"Very. Quite the cutie pie too," Mrs. Thompson replied as the key slid into the knob and worked the lock.

"Calm down there, Mary." Mr. Thompson chuckled. "I think he's a little too young for you."

Like a whisper, Becca cracked open the back door and slipped out. Behind me, the front lock clicked.

We are talking fractions of a second here. That's how close we got to being caught red-handed. Had I waited for Becca to start running her fingers through her hair in my explicit daydream in the bathroom, or had the camera caught on one more basement pipe, we would've been found out. I don't think you can play it any closer than that.

I followed Becca down the path, although not as gracefully, and as my dirty sneakers made first contact with the grass of the Thompsons' lawn, the hand squeezing my heart began to loosen. But it didn't completely let go. We weren't in the clear yet.

Becca closed the door as gently as she had opened it, her face a mask of seriousness and concentration, then her nails were digging into the soft skin of my bicep and she was pulling me into the bushes that divided the Thompson property from the house next door.

We bolted through backyards, ducking under clothing lines and hurdling patio furniture and swing sets.

When we came upon a chain-link fence the adrenaline made us scale them like world-class athletes. Hell, I didn't even care that I ripped the back of the shirt on one of the support poles.

An end finally in sight to our living nightmare, we crossed a dying garden overrun with weeds and came out near the intersection of Dart and Center.

It was here we stopped to catch our breath. The physical toll of our flight was catching up to me now. I leaned forward, hands on my knees, and tried to concentrate on inhaling through my nose and exhaling through my mouth, the way Owen had taught me after he had whooped my ass in basketball (all without breaking a sweat, I should add).

Pinpricks of stars floated at the edges of my vision, but surprisingly my head was clearer than it had felt in a long time.

After a minute or two, my breathing and heart rate somewhat under control, I straightened and looked at Becca. She had a smirk on her face as she made a noise I didn't immediately comprehend.

Because, in this situation, the noise made no sense.

She was laughing. Man, was she laughing.

"How?" was all I managed to say.

I couldn't tell you what that question was directed toward. How was she able to laugh? How did we get out of that without getting caught? Or how were we so stupid to go through with that idea in the first place?

I don't know.

Becca took a step to me. I watched her suspiciously. Had she lost her mind? There was this look in her eyes, equal parts scary and sexy. It was the kind of look that if she had flashed it to me in school, before I had ever talked to her or gotten to know her, I would've flinched away as if she had slapped my face.

"What is it?" I said.

But Becca wrapped me up in a hug and pressed her lips against my cheek. My neck popped with the force of the kiss, and there was a loud *smack* as she let go of me.

I stood there on an island of excitement, confusion, and hopelessness, stunned.

Hey, I know it wasn't anything to write home about, a simple peck on the cheek, but it was the first time a girl other than my mother or a distant relative had voluntarily kissed me.

And it lasted all of about a second, but it was the best second of my young life.

Becca carried on like nothing had happened.

Still slightly stunned, I brought my left hand up to my cheek and touched this now—in *my* mind, at least—sacred spot. The warmth of her lips lingered there, or so I imagined. In reality, it was probably the fire of embarrassment.

"Ali better not have ratted us out," she said. "If he did, I'm *so* kicking his ass."

"He didn't. He wouldn't," I said, stumbling over my words. "D-don't worry."

We started going south down Center Street, and a minute later, we were back on Whitehall Road.

I saw Ali pacing up and down the sidewalk between his house on Parkway and mine on the corner of Whitehall. He had his hands behind his head, like he was practicing for when the cops showed up. His bike was forgotten at the end of his driveway, the back tire still spinning. He must've rode around and looked for us after leaving the Thompsons'.

I whistled loudly, and he turned toward us. Becca waved.

Even from this distance, I could see the relief flooding through him. His rigid posture loosened as he took his cap off and armed sweat from his brow. It was warm out, but not stifling hot yet, like it would be in July and August. That sweat shining on his forehead was nervous sweat. I knew all about it —I was sweating myself.

"Oh, praise Allah!" he shouted, rushing toward us. "I was so worried. I whistled but I was not sure if you heard it. And then I engaged in conversation with the Thompsons for as long as I could—"

"You did great, man," I said, clapping him on the shoulder. "Thank you."

"That is...if you didn't rat us out," Becca said, her hand planted firmly on one hip, eyes narrowing.

Ali only looked confused. "Rat?"

"Tattle! Give us up to save your own ass!"

"Oh! No! Of course not! I tried to create a... how you say, *distraction*, that is all." Ali smiled. "One thing I have learned through observation of my own is that the people of Ohio, especially the males, have one consistent weakness in conversation. Their house could be on fire and they would still stop and indulge in this weakness."

"What is it?" I asked.

"All you have to do is bring up a professional American football team by the name of the Cleveland Browns. The people here will talk about them until they are blueberry in the face."

"Blueberry?" Becca said and chuckled. "You mean *blue* in the face."

"Ah, yes. They will talk until they are *blue* in the face. Then, if you bring up another American football team, the Pittsburgh Steelers, call them inept, and how this upcoming year is *finally* the Browns' year, you can earn nearly any Ohioan's trust."

I nodded, impressed.

"If that fails," Ali continued, "you can do the same for another American football team, this one of the collegiate variety—"

"Ohio State," I guessed.

"Correct." Ali smiled. "Who also have a nemesis reminiscent of the Browns and Steelers rivalry in the Michigan Wolverines."

Ali was pretty pleased with himself, and to be honest, he had every right to be.

What he said was true. The people in Northeast Ohio loved their Cleveland sports teams, especially the Browns, which was something I never understood.

Football wasn't a favorite sport of mine, but living in Pickwick, it couldn't help but reach you through osmosis. People would talk about it at the supermarket, and teachers would come to class on casual Fridays decked out in Browns gear (aside from Mr. DeLuca, the school staff's lone die-hard Steelers fan).

I'm sure Owen could've explained it to me better, but from what I picked up, the Cleveland Browns absolutely sucked.

That 2008 season, the first during my time there, the team posted a record of four wins and twelve losses and wasn't even close enough to catch a whiff of the playoffs.

But even when all hope was lost, the Northeast Ohioans stayed strong. They never turned on their team, they continued hating the Steelers and Big Ben Roethlisberger, and they stayed in the stadium for their Brownies until the final whistle echoed through the mostly quiet stadium.

There was always next year was the unofficial Cleveland sports motto.

I truly don't know how they did it. I don't know how they stayed so optimistic in such a gray and cold place (at least in Pennsylvania we had winning teams to help us through the harsh winters).

To this day, I still don't know how they did it. And although I didn't stay in Ohio long after that summer of 2009, I am proud to have called myself an Ohioan for that small bit of time.

"So that is what I did," Ali continued. "I brought up the Cleveland Browns to Mr. Thompson. I asked him if the team should start Brady Quinn or Derek Anderson at quarterback, and Mr. Thompson rambled on about how Quinn was what he called a 'homer,' having grown up in the area, and how he would never forgive Derek Anderson for throwing four interceptions in a 2007 loss to the Cincinnati Bengals, a game that would potentially gotten the Browns into the playoffs had they won it, and Mrs. Thompson elbowed him and told him to quit his crying about that and move on!" Ali shrugged. "See, once you get them started, all you have to do is nod your head and appear to be listening. It is as simple as that."

Becca and me nodded lazily and mumbled an "Uh-huh" and a "Yeah" and a "Definitely" before Ali caught on to the joke. It didn't take him long—he was getting better at that. Then Becca and I started laughing.

"Yes, yes, very funny. Let's all laugh at Ali Bu Ali Al-Kareem, the eternal butt of jokes." He waved his hand. "Now enough of this nonsense. Did you find any evidence?"

I held up my video camera. "Well, we're about to find out."

Back in Ali's living room, I opened the camera's viewfinder, and Ali and Becca crowded around me.

As I hit the play button, Becca said, "Wait. Do you have a TV or something? I can hardly see on that tiny screen."

Consumer technology was a few years away from the 4K televisions that would eventually become a staple in many homes, but we didn't need 4K then. We just needed something that could stretch the picture without losing too much of the 1080p quality.

"There is a television downstairs," Ali said. "It is quite old, and I am not sure it works, but it is much bigger than your miniature screen."

"Hey," I said, "it's not the size of the boat, it's the motion—"

Becca elbowed me. "Go get it."

So Ali and I did. It was pretty dated, but not as dated as he had made it out to be. We tried it in the basement first to make sure it worked and then lugged it upstairs. With how clunky and heavy it was, I'm surprised we didn't kill ourselves in the process.

We set it on the floor near an outlet in the living room, and I plugged it in. The dusty screen showed snowy static. As I searched through my bag for the right A/V cables, Becca closed the blinds and turned the deadbolt on the front door.

"What are you doing?" Ali said. "If my brother or my father arrives home to find the door locked and the blinds drawn while I have a female in the house, I will be murdered."

"If the wrong person sees what's on this video, you could be murdered," I said. "Pick your poison. Death by daddy or death by a pissed-off werewolf."

Ali sighed resignedly.

"Yeah, exactly," Becca said. "Now play the tape, John."

"It's actually not a tape," I began. "It's digital—"

Becca frowned. "Oh, shut up, nerd."

I plugged all the wires in and turned the camera on. The battery was flashing red, but there was enough juice to get us through at least one viewing before it needed a charge.

On the screen, the static disappeared, replaced by heavy darkness. Auto night mode kicked on a few seconds later. I pressed the Vol. + button and heard loud *clunks* come through the television's speakers and the distant hushed syllables of Becca's and my words as we argued from above in the bathroom.

The darkness lasted another twenty seconds, and then the lens passed a series of bright white PVC pipes. There was a jumble of sound as the camera scraped past them and then a *twang* as it dropped and the belt went taut.

Dangling there, the lens struggled to gain focus and we couldn't see much of anything besides a bunch of blurred shapes.

"C'mon, c'mon," I said.

"Your camera's busted," Becca said. "All that for a blurry—"

I patted the camera, as if it would make a difference to something that was already in the past, and said, "You got this. I believe in you, buddy."

"Oh, brother." Becca rolled her eyes and pushed off the arm of the couch.

"There!" Ali said. "Look!"

The auto-focus finally adjusted. That along with the night mode made for a decently clear picture of a basement as plain and as dull as the rest of the inside of the house had been.

Becca laughed. "There's a washer and dryer, a basket of dirty laundry. Oh! And look, a menacing, *evil* broom standing up in the corner right there!" She sighed. "The little faith I had in what you think we saw last night is going…going…going…"

"It doesn't make sense," I said. "Mr. Thompson was there. No way it was random. *No way.*"

Becca stretched both of her arms high above her head and yawned. "All right, now that's settled and we've wasted a bunch of time already, can we please get back to working on the movie? I really don't want to be out as late as we were yesterday."

"Why else would Mr. Thompson be there?" I said. "Why else would a man who goes to bed at eight every evening be walking through the woods a ways behind his house after midnight?"

"Maybe he needed some fresh air," Becca said. "I don't know. It's pretty evident now that it's none of our business. Instead of pointing the finger at him, maybe we should *actually* be grateful for him, you know, for saving our asses from that animal."

"From that *werewolf*," I growled.

"Give it a break, John. I know you're still young and all, but life is not a horror movie—"

"Uh…" Ali was saying behind us, neither Becca nor me paying much attention to him. "My friends…my friends…you need to see this."

"I think maybe you need to start wearing glasses," I said. "And what about the thing *you* saw by the dumpster at the hardware store?"

Faced with the harsh truth of the Thompsons' normal basement, I was growing desperate.

Was I projecting? Was this just me trying to find some other explanation for my brother's death? Was it so hard for me to accept that someone as great as Owen Carver could accidentally be killed? That he could actually get drunk and wander off into the woods, take a bad fall, and die?

"What I saw back then," Becca said, "is certainly looking more and more like what I originally thought, isn't it? A mother-loving homeless guy! A drug addict! A hobo!" She spread her eyes open with the thumb and index finger of each hand. "Just look, John! That's all you have to do! Pickwick isn't perfect. People like that slip through the cracks and come through town now and then—"

"Shut up!" Ali shouted. "Both of you shut up!"

Becca and I turned and stared at him.

He was standing in front of the screen, blocking

the picture. All I could see besides the fuzziness of the whitewashed, night-visioned walls was the word PAUSE in the top right corner.

Ali stepped aside. "Look at the television! I demand you look at it right now!"

"*Holy shit,*" I said.

That was all I could say.

CHAPTER 11
TALE OF THE TAPE

STILL HANGING from Becca's belt, the camera had spun around and showed the other side of the basement.

In the far right corner of the room stood two walls of iron bars. A thick chain with an attached padlock dangled from the handle. The padlock was easily as big as my fist.

"What the hell is that? Is that a jail cell?" Becca said, her nose almost pressed against the TV screen.

Inside the cell was a thin mattress and an overturned bucket. Stuffing coiled out of a score of slashes in the mattress, and the bucket was covered in congealed...*something.* Blood or vomit or excrement, I wasn't sure.

"I think it is," I said, grimacing. "Why would he have a cell in his basement? His *locked* basement?"

"Perhaps he is holding a hostage," Ali said.

"Well, if he is, he isn't anymore," I said.

"Could be that our pal Mr. Thompson actually *is* into some freaky sex shit," Becca said. "Like BDSM stuff—chains and whips and gimp suits."

"That's a possibility," I said, but the thought of Mr. Thompson dressed up like the gimp in *Pulp Fiction* had me wishing for my own puke bucket. "I don't see any sex toys, though. If this is a kink, it's a freaking weird one."

"Which is exactly what makes it a kink," Becca said.

I nodded at Ali. "Can you hit play?" For about thirty seconds the camera swiveled back and forth, not offering anything else to back up our theories—either that Mr. Thompson was a werewolf or that he and his wife were into kinky sex.

"Your camera operating skills are lacking," Becca said as we watched. She backed away and straightened. "God, it's making me nauseous—"

The camera jerked, the sudden bounce causing it to nosedive.

"Wait!" I said. "Rewind it a few frames and pause."

"Frames?"

"Just hit the rewind button."

Ali did.

"There! Pause it!" I tapped the screen. "You see that?"

Slowly, the others approached the television.

"Is that—?" Becca began.

"Blood," Ali finished.

I tapped the screen again, this time hard enough for it to sting the tip of my finger. "That's not all. Does *that* look familiar to you, Ali?"

Ali's mouth opened. His eyes grew cartoonishly big. "Oh my…" he gasped.

My nail rested a centimeter below a nail of a different kind—a *claw*, rather. The claw of some great beast.

A werewolf's claw.

"Are you sure?" Becca was saying as she squinted at the television. "That could be—"

"We're sure," I said. "That thing didn't come from any normal animal. I mean, look at it! It's like a scythe. I know you didn't see what we saw as well as we did, but Ali and I had front-row seats to that horror show."

I took over the operating duties from Ali and hit play on the video camera. Squinting at the quivering footage, I paused it again as the viewpoint shifted down. This time we saw the floor leading to the cage.

"Christ," I whispered.

"What—what happened there?" Ali said, leaning forward.

"Looks like roadkill," Becca said.

I shook my head. "No. Not roadkill."

"Then what?" Becca's cheeks had paled.

"If I had to guess, I'd say we're looking at the aftermath of the transformation back to human." I pointed to the clumps of coarse brown fur mingled with gooey clumps of blood and discharge.

"So what, he loses all the fur when the sun comes up or something?" Becca rubbed her forehead. "God, what the hell am I saying? This is crazy."

"I read about it in one of the books I got from the library. During the transformation, most of the fur is absorbed back into the body, but a werewolf is part animal after all. They shed like animals, and during the 'regression phase'—that's what the author called it—the human part tries really hard to reject the beast. The result is"—I tapped the screen—"this."

Becca laughed and quickly covered her mouth.

"What?" I asked.

"I'm sorry. I'm not trying to be an ass. I just got this funny image in my head of Mr. Thompson dragging his half-dog butt across the rug."

Ali laughed.

I wrinkled my nose. "Okay, that's not something I wanted to picture."

"He probably lifts his leg on that fire hydrant outside of his house too," Becca added and chuckled again.

I pointed to the screen. "All jokes aside, is that enough evidence for you?"

Becca folded her arms over her chest. "Um…I don't know. It's weird, that's for sure."

"Yeah, that's an understatement."

"The way I understand it," Ali said, pacing around the living room, "there are three explanations. One, Mr. Thompson is the werewolf. Two, *Mrs.* Thompson is the werewolf. Or three, both of the Thompsons are *harboring* a werewolf."

"Like a secret werewolf love child?" Becca said.

"Ooh, hey, that's a cool title. If you ever do a romance-horror movie, John, there it is."

I rolled my eyes. "Nice."

"A child?" Ali said. "I am not sure of that."

"I doubt they're hiding a werewolf," I said. "I've never seen anyone else at their house before, and I've spent a good amount of time around there. It's one of them, gotta be. The cage is for protection when the full moon's out. Lock whoever it is before the change and save lives."

"And it saves whichever spouse *isn't* the creature," Becca said. "Interesting."

"I do doubt Mrs. Thompson is a werewolf," Ali said.

Becca scowled. "What? Why? Because she's a woman?"

"No. Now, I do not mean to be sexist," he said, "but the beast I laid eyes upon last night was too large to be Mrs. Thompson. I spoke with her recently. She is of a small frame and a kind heart."

"Still a little bit sexist," Becca mumbled.

"Okay, okay," I said before things got out of hand, "whatever the case, we're going to find out."

"Yeah…I guess we are," Becca said. She backed away from the TV and leaned against the bare, eggshell colored wall opposite the front door. "But how do we do that?"

I didn't answer. I didn't exactly know. Those chapters were left out of the books I had borrowed, and there was nothing on the internet besides the usual Hollywood bullshit.

"My uncle's a vet in Stratton. Bet I can get a discount on some werewolf euthanasia. At least it'll be humane, you know." She chuckled.

I frowned, but not at Becca's joke. I frowned because my mind was kicking into gear. The seed of an idea I had subconsciously planted while reading the old library books in the park earlier that day had begun to blossom.

"Becca..." Ali whispered, tilting his head toward her. "I think John has had enough of our teasing."

"Oh c'mon, I'm just joking!" Becca nudged me. Too deep in thought, I barely felt it. "John? You okay?"

My mind continued running. I was thinking about the words *Vet* and *werewolf* and *euthanasia.*

"John?" Ali said, genuine concern in his voice.

Becca waved her hand in front of my face, and that was when I heard a click in my head, the sound of the last puzzle piece snapping into place.

I darted for my backpack leaning against the leg of the bare coffee table. I lugged it back over to the TV as Ali and Becca looked at me in confusion.

"What are you doing?" Ali asked.

To Becca I said, "Is your uncle really a veterinarian?"

"Well, he's my uncle by marriage, and apparently that marriage isn't doing so hot. But yeah, he's a vet. He has his own practice right off 91. Dr. Kressler." She raised an eyebrow. "Wait, why? I was just joking about the werewolf euthanasia thing. I'm gonna guess it wouldn't work that way."

"Nobody knows how it works," I said as I pulled out one of the books I'd gotten from the library, *The Lycanthropy Curse*, and flipped to a page I had marked with a sticky note. "Here," I said. "Listen: *'There is a wealth of similarities between the lycanthropy affliction and that of the rabies virus. As with the virus, an increase in body temperature is often followed by symptoms such as nausea and vomiting, an inability to control basic motor functions, excitement, a fear of water, and the loss of consciousness. Those suffering from lycanthropy have all but the fear of water. In fact, those who've been cursed by the wolf do not fear anything so far as we know. It is as if supernatural animalistic urge overtakes any semblance of the human it has possessed.'"*

Becca stared, Ali nodded thoughtfully, and I waited a couple seconds for a response neither offered.

"You following?"

Ali shook his head; Becca said, "Umm...not really. I mean, 'semblance,' 'affliction,' 'lycanthropy?' How about you try again but this time speak *English*, please?"

"Ali, do you have internet?"

"I do."

"Where's the computer?"

"It's in my father's office off of the dining room, but we can't—"

Before he could finish his sentence, I was already there. The office was big but cluttered. A stark contrast to the sterile look of the rest of the house.

I slid into a chair, the back of my knees squeaking against the leather, and I fired up a clunky Gateway. There was no password to bypass, thankfully. Once in, I was greeted by a blurry background picture of Ali's whole family. Ali was kneeling with a few other boys his age, their arms out, silly expressions on their faces.

"John, I mean it! We can't use my father's personal property—" He stopped and examined the background photo, his eyebrows rising toward his hairline.

"Nice pic," I said.

Ali continued to stare.

"Are you okay?" Becca asked him, putting her hand on his shoulder.

"I—um, yes, I am. I just remember taking this photograph and my father yelling at my cousins, my brother, and myself for ruining it. I was sure he had deleted it."

"Guess not," I said. "He's probably not as much of a hard-ass as you think. He obviously loves you, and that's more than I can say for my dad."

"How touching…" Becca said. "Now what the hell is the point of this? You can't just read some crazy sentences from a weird book and then run off to check your MySpace."

"Hold on." I opened the browser and headed to Google. A few minutes later, I had found the info I needed.

"Basically," I said, "the theory is that the werewolf curse, the *affliction*, is a form of the rabies virus. A *way stronger* form. But the book I read from was originally written in like the 1850s."

"Okay?" Becca said. "That's not helping."

I pointed to the computer screen, which showed

a webpage dedicated to rabies. "The rabies vaccine wasn't developed until 1885, almost thirty years *after* the publication of the book. Unfortunately, the author died in 1870. So he was never able to test his theory."

"Or you know," Becca said, "this could all be bullshit."

"That's harsh, yeah, but possible." I shrugged. "This is a theory, that's all. And right now, that's all we have to go on."

"What about silver?" Ali said. "Or wolfsbane?"

"Movie stuff?" I said.

"Oh no, here comes another nerd rant…" Becca mumbled.

I ignored her. "Silver got popular after it was used in *The Wolf Man*, but the idea that it wards off evil goes back way longer. It's a trope."

"Trope?" Ali said.

"Ali, what have you done?" Becca pulled at her blonde locks. "I graduated from school. I'm done with lectures."

"Just listen," I said. "Basically, it's a common theme or image you see in certain genres. How many romance movies are there where the main characters don't live happily ever after? Virtually none, right? Because *Happily Ever After* is a trope.

There's even tropes in horror movies. You pop a *Friday the 13th* movie into the DVD player and you know you're about to watch a bunch of teens smoke weed, drink alcohol, and have premarital sex for the first act of the movie. Then Jason'll come along and chop them to pieces in the second act, and then the final girl, usually the one who didn't join in on all the sex, drugs, and rock and roll, has to fight for her life throughout the third act and climax." I took in a deep breath. "A trope is *expectations*. It's a storytelling tool. It's not science. What *The Lycanthropy Curse* is talking about here is science."

"Ancient science," Becca said. "Civil War-era science."

"What else do we have?"

Ali pushed his hat back and scratched beneath his dark bangs. "Okay, but what do rabies and the vaccine have to do with it?"

"Becca's uncle," I said. "He's gotta have the vaccine at his office. One of the first things they do to kittens and puppies when they go to the vet is give them the rabies vaccine, yeah? If Becca can get it—and I mean as much as you can, Becca—and we inject the werewolf with it, we might be able to cure it."

"Or…it may kill it," Ali whispered. His bottom lip trembled.

I thought of Owen. I thought of those terrible claws I had seen last night tearing him apart, those fangs ripping into his throat, and shrugged.

My voice was flat when I said, "Either way, it's a win-win." I looked at Becca. "Can you get your hands on some?"

"I guess I can try."

"What if you're wrong?" Ali said. "What if it does not kill or cure? What if it does nothing?"

"We'll cross that bridge when we get to it."

"Perhaps there are truths in the movies, John. Perhaps silver is deadly and wolfsbane is poisonous. If werewolves are actually real and not some fictitious creation—which we now know is the case—then why can't these solutions also be real? I see no problem in having a plan to fall back on."

"Ali," I said, "movies are my religion, but they're not my reality. We don't live in a world where there are three distinct acts. We live in a world where nothing's guaranteed. But the closest we can get to a guarantee is science."

Ali nodded. I could tell he wasn't convinced.

"Where would I even get a silver bullet or a gun for that matter?" I said.

"It doesn't have to be a bullet, does it?"

I put both of my hands up. "That's the thing, dude. *I don't know.* Have you ever seen *An American Werewolf in London?*"

"I do not believe so."

"First of all, you should. But basically, the main character gets turned into a werewolf. I think he kills his best friend, and then the ghost of said friend haunts him for a good chunk of the movie, trying to get him to off himself. The main character asks if he has to do it with a silver bullet, and the best friend says something like, 'Oh, be serious!'"

"Your point?" Becca said.

"My point is, how can we trust the movies? Every film establishes its own rules and guidelines. They make them up!"

"Yes, I understand," Ali said.

"Good." I sighed, peering through the lone window on the far wall. Night would fall in an hour or two. Another early summer's day in the books. "So…this whole situation might be bleak, but we do have one thing going for us."

"What's that?" Becca said.

"The moon. Next full one won't be for like another thirty days, right?"

"I guess we should thank God for small miracles."

The tension in the small office began to fade.

"Exactly," I said, "because we got a film of our own to finish." I smiled. "Now let's get back to work."

It hadn't crossed our minds that the correlation between full moons and werewolves might've at least been somewhat exaggerated too.

Then again, we were already in *way* over our heads. I don't blame us.

CHAPTER 12
AN UNINVITED GUEST

AFTER FILMING a couple of scenes in Ali's house, the three of us went out to his backyard, which was nice with a patio, sparse furniture, and an old-looking grill—all left by the previous tenants.

Ali pulled up some lawn chairs and offered us cans of Coca-Cola. The late breeze stirred my hair as I sat back, sipped my ice-cold pop and took in the darkening sky.

It amazes me to this day how we were able to put all the werewolf business aside and work on *Creature*.

At the same time, it also doesn't. Working on that short film was my escape. *Our* escape. For me, my mind went blank and thoughts of Owen were muted.

For Ali, I think it was his family he worried about. His mother in Oman. His father here.

Becca, she was more of an enigma. Back then, I found it hard to believe someone like her could have any worries or fears or anxieties. She was also pretty good at hiding it. But like Ali and I, she was human. She wanted to get away from this town and make something of herself.

Becca yawned. "This is pretty nice, huh?"

"What is?" I said.

"I don't know, just hanging out and doing nothing."

"I agree, it is quite lovely," Ali said.

"Yeah, it is." I held up Coke. "I feel like we should toast."

"To what?" Becca asked.

I shrugged. "To *Creature*."

Ali raised his drink. "And to new friends."

Becca started laughing "And to killing werewolves."

"Cheers," I said.

Our Cokes sloshed as our cans clinked together.

"I'm glad I agreed to do this," Becca said. "The movie. And you know what? I don't really care if we win."

"It would be nice, though," I said.

"Yeah. But even if we don't, we aren't leaving empty-handed."

"Oh no," I said, nodding at Ali. "Tough Becca is getting all sentimental on us."

She flipped me the bird, and I smiled at her.

"It's just nice to hang out with guys who aren't trying to constantly get in my pants."

"Yeah," I said, "I hate when guys try to get in my pants."

Becca snorted, then she rubbed her nose and started cough-laughing. "You almost made me spit up my Coke, you ass!"

"Sorry, I'm just saying—"

"HEY!" a voice interrupted, coming from the direction of the gate by the garage. "What the hell were you kids doing in my house?"

My whole body froze. The air in my lungs evaporated.

The voice belonged to Mr. Thompson, and gone was his polite but slightly timid demeanor.

He smashed the bar on the gate with the heel of his hand. It shot upward and banged against the support pole.

His hair was frazzled, in tufts at the sides, and the strands he usually combed over the top pointed in every direction. His clothes seemed baggier too, loose against his thin frame.

Looking into his face was like looking into the face of Death. Dark semi-circles stood out beneath his eyes. Razor-sharp cheekbones poked through his paper-thin pale skin.

Was this the aftereffects of a transformation? A hangover of some kind?

Neither Ali nor me said anything. I don't think we could've—we were too scared.

But thank the Good Lord that Becca was there. She screwed her face up in confusion, jerked upward in her chair, and said, "Whoa, man! What the hell do you think you're doing? You can't be coming at us like this! Leave or I'll call the cops!"

Mr. Thompson smiled sickly as he charged across the backyard toward the patio. "You left the window open."

He beelined across the lawn, each step filled with a terrible purpose. I realized then that Mr. Thompson had no plans to call the police or tell our parents.

He wanted to teach us a lesson himself.

Owen's voice filled my head: *Put up or shut up, little brother.*

As much as I wanted to bolt, I didn't. This was

my fault. I saw no reason my friends had to go down for my idea and actions.

"I thought better of you, John," Mr. Thompson said. "I really did." His hands were balled into fists. The last bit of sunlight reflected off the sweat coating his brow.

I stood from my chair, an alien anger surging through my body.

I wanted to be a normal teenager. I wanted to enjoy my summer and not have to worry about werewolves or think about my dead brother.

Most of all, I wanted to be left alone.

"John...what are you doing?" Ali whispered. His chair raked over the concrete as he stood beside me.

"Can't say I'm surprised," Mr. Thompson said, a mere dozen steps away from us now. "Once you start hanging out with"—he glared first at Ali and then Becca—"a *towelhead* and a *whore*, things can only go downhill from there."

My ears began to ring. "What the hell did you say about my friends?"

"You heard me," Mr. Thompson said. He puffed his chest out. Taller than me, I had to look up to him. He reached down and grabbed beneath the collar of my t-shirt, his thin fingers pinching the skin of my chest.

"Hey!" Becca shouted. "Let him go!"

Unprepared for this reaction, the fight had gone out of me.

As a teenager, there are fewer things more alarming than an adult stooping to your level. I think because when an adult strikes a kid, you can't help but think this is an adult with nothing to lose.

Weakly, I beat at Mr. Thompson's hands but did no more damage than gnats at a picnic.

He shook me. "You punk-ass kids think it's okay to run around the neighborhood and do as you please? Think you can break into *my* house? Go through *my* stuff? No. No. NO!"

I closed my eyes, preparing for the pain. When you were bullied as much as I was, you knew when it was best to close your eyes. It didn't make it hurt less, but I preferred not to see the fists flying at my face. "Well, we're gonna change that today—"

I heard a hard *clunk,* and then Mr. Thompson groaned like a drunk submitting to the effects of an all-night bender.

He let go of me.

I stumbled backward, pinwheeling my arms for balance. When I got my footing, I saw Ali standing next to Mr. Thompson. He was holding a decorative garden stone. Painted on it was an American flag made to look like it was waving in the wind.

Now it had a fresh streak of red smeared across it.

Mr. Thompson brought a hand up to the right side of his head, above his eyebrow, and looked at his fingers. They were wet with blood.

"*Wuhh—*" he managed before he collapsed half on the patio and half in the grass.

Becca, Ali, and I stared at each other before our eyes found the unmoving Mr. Thompson. We stared for what felt like a long time.

In the distance, thunder rolled. The atmosphere had obviously taken a nosedive, and now, for some strange reason, a storm was on the horizon.

It was me who broke the silence. "Whoa..."

Ali flung the rock like it was on fire. "I panicked," he said.

Becca knelt and pressed two fingers on Mr. Thompson's neck. "He's not dead. We're okay."

"What do we do?" Ali had his hands on the top of his head.

"It was self-defense, man. Relax," I said, but I knew that would never hold up for Ali.

I examined the cut on Mr. Thompson's head. It

was long but shallow. Not life-threatening, but enough to send him to the ground and cause some damage.

"Do you have rope?" I asked. "Something we can tie him up with?"

"What? Are you crazy?" Ali screeched.

"The full moon was last night," Becca said, eyeing me warily. "He won't change."

"What we are talking about is kidnapping!" Ali whisper-shouted.

"It's precautionary," I said. "He's gonna wake up eventually and he's gonna be *pissed*." I put an arm around Ali. "Thank you, by the way."

"I didn't mean to—"

I squeezed his shoulder. "It's okay, man. Relax. Just relax. We'll figure this out."

Ali inhaled deeply, exhaled, and then nodded.

I looked down at the unconscious Mr. Thompson. "But first, we're going to get some information."

We dragged Mr. Thompson into the garage and wrestled him into a folding chair.

The garage, home of Ali's father's old but slick

Mercedes Benz, was empty save for a few boxes on shelves, a snow shovel, rusty tools left behind by the last family who lived here, and half a dozen bags of weed eater.

The only window was set high in the southwestern wall, offering a distant glimpse of my street. If I climbed those shelves and looked out, I might be able to see my house down to the left. My mother was working and wouldn't be home until late.

Mr. Thompson's hands were bound tightly with bungee cables and his torso down to his legs were duct taped about a thousand times over. We had used an entire roll and a half, all the tape Ali had.

The whole time, of course, Ali protested. Becca hadn't. She only watched with an air of strange fascination, probably wondering how a shy kid like me could go from being barely able to speak to her to *this*.

The answer was simple, though. It was because of my brother. Avenging him, finding out the truth —those were my sole motivators.

"What about his wife?" Becca said. "She's gonna think something's up."

"True, yes. That's why we'll have to be quick."

"Christ," Becca said.

"You said it," Ali agreed.

"You can leave if you want," I said. "This is between Thompson and me."

"This is my house! I cannot leave!"

"We're in too deep now, Ali," Becca said. "Any way you flip it, we're part of this." She smiled. "Isn't that exciting?"

"You're crazy," I told her.

"Yeah. Maybe a little."

I shook my head and looked at Mr. Thompson. His head lolled as he shifted and grunted something.

We all took a big step away from him as his eyes opened to slits. He took in his surroundings, and once they proved unfamiliar, his eyes widened.

"…the fuck?"

Showtime.

Ali scuttled out of Mr. Thompson's line of sight and took refuge behind the bags of weed eater against the back wall. Becca stayed where she was on Mr. Thompson's right side. He didn't notice her; instead, he focused on me and lunged.

The binds made sure he got nowhere. Veins from his neck bulged and quivered like fat snakes. His face turned a dark reddish-purple as if he had forgotten to breathe.

"You little shit! I'll fucking kill you. Do you realize who you fucked with?" he growled.

I spoke calmly: "Mr. Thompson, all I want is the truth. Okay?"

He lunged again. The chair teetered but stayed upright.

"I understand you're angry and your head is probably hurting, but I don't want there to be any more pain. That's why I did this. That's why I broke into your house."

At that, Mr. Thompson only seemed to get angrier.

Here I was standing before him, a skinny, weaponless teenager, and I wondered what the hell I was doing.

Think about Owen, I told myself. *You're doing this for your brother.*

"I don't want anyone to get hurt," I said. "But"—I stepped over to the shelf and grabbed a rusty wrench—"I'm not completely opposed to violence to get what I want in this situation." I knelt down so I was eye to eye with Mr. Thompson. "Are we good?"

Realizing he couldn't bust out of the duct tape and cords, Mr. Thompson had stopped trying, but there was still murder in his eyes. He blinked for the first time since coming to, and then he nodded.

"All right," I said. "No sugar-coating. No beating around the bush. Who is the werewolf? Is it you?"

His eyebrows drew downward, making a soft popping sound as dried blood crackled in his hair. "The *what?*"

Behind him, Ali began to pray in Arabic.

I was undeterred. "A werewolf, Mr. Thompson. A person who changes into a big wolf-like creature when the moon is full."

"Like the supernatural kind," Becca said. "And do you frequently eat from dumpsters, or was that just, like, a one-off thing?"

I shot her a warning look. She grinned.

Mr. Thompson sighed. "You kids have lost your goddamn minds."

"This isn't the time to play around," I said.

"I'm not a werewolf, okay? Is that what you want to hear?" The anger in his voice had subsided. Now he sounded concerned…for me?

I didn't understand.

"You were there last night," I said, "when we saw it in the woods. And you have a cage in your basement, and there was hair and blood and a claw down there."

"What? I don't know what kind of sick game you're playing, John, but I want no part in it."

"So it's a sex thing?" Becca said. "The cage, I mean."

"Becca…" I said.

"What? I'm interested!"

"Do you hear yourselves?" Mr. Thompson said. "A werewolf?" He squinted. "Are you on drugs, John? I know it's rumored your brother was—"

"Don't you talk about my brother!" I shouted, my voice shaking.

"John, please. I need to get home. My wife, she has not been feeling well. If she wakes up and sees I'm not home this late, she'll worry, and that will only hurt her worse. Do you understand?"

"So you didn't tell her about us breaking in?" Becca asked. She stepped forward.

Mr. Thompson tilted his head. "What—? I, uh, no. I didn't want to upset her."

"Interesting." Becca tapped her bottom lip and stared at me. "What's wrong with your wife? She seemed fine on your little evening stroll earlier."

"A bug," Mr. Thompson said matter-of-factly. He turned to me. "It's been bothering her on and off for a few weeks now. Please, I'd like to get back to her and make sure she is okay."

His change of attitude felt off. How could he calm down so quickly? It made no sense. I decided I had to keep the pressure on.

"My brother," I said. "Did you kill him? The night he died, it was a full moon. I double-checked."

"John, I am sorry about what happened to your brother, but I had nothing to do with it. I promise you. Now please, let me go."

Thunder grumbled louder, the budding storm closer now. Mr. Thompson's eyes drifted to his left, and he stole a glance out the window where the moon, nearly as full as it was last night, shone through the swollen clouds.

"I will never speak of this again. And I should've never rushed at you like I did. I was just so angry, but I'm clearheaded now. Please untie me."

I nodded to the window. "No full moon tonight. It looks like it, but it's not."

"John," Ali whispered. "I think we should let him go. He said he will not speak of this."

"That's bullshit," Becca said.

"Exactly," I said.

"Please…" Mr. Thompson moaned. "It's getting late—"

A car roared down the street.

At first I hoped what I heard was thunder, because that sounded familiar. It sounded like the Mustang that tore through the school parking lot at the end of every day, tires screeching, music blaring. That Mustang belonged to Ryan Kensington.

I went to the side door, cracked it, and peeked out.

Through a curtain of falling rain, I saw that the driveway was empty, but sure enough an old cherry-red Mustang was parked nearby on the street, its engine idling.

In it were two figures. I would've bet my life they were Ryan Kensington and Dave Rivers.

"Is someone here?" Ali said.

I nodded at Becca. "It's your boyfriend."

"Ryan?"

"Yeah. He needs to go. He can't see this."

A moment later, Ryan shouted her name from the driveway. "Are you here, babe? Listen, I just wanna talk!"

Before I could even think about taping Mr. Thompson's mouth shut, he began to scream.

"HEY! HELP ME! I'M BEING HELD

AGAINST MY WILL! HELP! HELP! HEEEEELP—!"

I dropped the wrench and bolted over to him. The wrench clanged off of the painted concrete floor, reverberating along the walls. I clamped my right and left hand over Mr. Thompson's lips. *"Shut up."*

He kept screaming but his words were muffled by my palm. I looked over my shoulder and said to Becca, "Get them out of here!" Then to Ali, I said, "Can you find more tape—OUCH! *WHAT THE FUCK!*"

An explosion of pain ripped through my hand. Mr. Thompson had bit the fleshy underside of my thumb, and I staggered away.

"Hey, in the garage!" Dave Rivers said.

The scuffle of their shoes over the drive grew louder.

"What the hell is going on in there?" Ryan Kensington said.

Ali rushed the door and hit it with his shoulder. He had taken off like a rocket, but his small frame was no match for the athletic build of a guy like Ryan, and Ali bounced off and fell back on his ass.

Ryan stepped in like nothing had happened. He stared at us and our hostage with blank-faced confusion. Dave, behind him, was smiling. He must've thought this was a joke. A middle-aged guy duct taped to a chair, head bleeding; me bent over and squeezing my throbbing hand, a discarded rusty wrench at my feet, Becca watching from the side, and Ali splayed out on the floor.

Yeah, that was one hell of a joke.

"Hi Ryan," Becca said. "Listen, I'm a little busy right now, but I'll shoot you a text when we're finished up here."

"What in the holy fuck are you doing?" Ryan said.

"Dude, just leave," I said.

"Jesus Christ, Carver. I knew you were a freak but I didn't think you were *this* weird. And what are you doing here with him, Becca?"

"It's for a movie," Becca said.

Ali picked himself up and dusted off his robes.

"Don't listen to them!" Mr. Thompson said. "First they assaulted me, and then they kidnapped me. Now they're going to kill me! I don't know what is wrong with them. I think—I think they're Satanists or something."

"Becca…" Ryan said.

"He's just really in character," Becca said. She

kicked Mr. Thompson in the shin. "It's okay, Mr. Thompson. John said cut. You can cool it."

"Where's the camera?" Dave said.

"Rehearsal," I said. "Going through the scene before we shoot it." I thought I sounded convincing enough.

Becca stepped forward and grabbed the hem of Ryan's shirt. He pushed her away, disgusted, and walked toward Mr. Thompson, whose eyes were now wet and shiny with relief.

"We're not idiots," Ryan said.

I got between them, put both of my hands up. "Please, Ryan. You really can't be here, okay? This is—"

I grunted as Ryan's large hand palmed my face and pushed me to the side with incredible force.

Stumbling, I rammed into the shelves beneath the window. A cascade of dust and dirt fell into my eyes and mouth.

"Dave, c'mon. Help me get this old dude out of here."

"Ryan!" Becca said. "I said I'd text you."

"Just tell them the truth," Ali said. "We can use more allies."

This got Dave and Ryan's attention, and a cold silence settled over the garage.

"What I said is the truth!" Mr. Thompson suddenly shouted, the chair jumping an inch off the floor as he struggled to get free.

"The truth," Becca said, her voice defeated, "is that we think Mr. Thompson here is a werewolf, or at the very least *knows* about a werewolf." She chuckled. "Yeah, it sounds—"

Dave and Ryan looked at each other and burst into deep, raucous laughter.

Still dazed, I clambered back to my feet, stepping into a shaft of white light from the moon. Outside, the storm had broken open. Now it was raging.

As they laughed, Ryan took a pocket knife out from his shorts and sliced the duct tape around Mr. Thompson's legs, while Dave worked on the bungee cords around his wrists.

"Thank you, thank you, thank you!" Mr. Thompson was saying, shaking free of the tape and standing. "A thousand times thank you." Now up, he power-walked toward the door.

"Wait," Ryan called after him. "You want us to get the police or an ambulance or something? Your head looks pretty bad."

Mr. Thompson stuck up a hand in a hold-on

gesture but kept on walking until he disappeared into the storm.

Ryan looked at Becca. She shrugged and chuckled. "I told you, he takes his character *very* seriously."

"This is so fucking weird," Ryan said.

Dave touched his brow. "All that blood looked real, man."

"Ali's a hell of a makeup artist," Becca said.

"Whatever," Ryan said. He slouched, casting a sideways glance at me, and then lowered his voice. "Can we talk, Bec? I'm miserable without us."

"There was never an us. There was just you using me for sex."

"C'mon, that's not true—"

"Ryan, go home. Please."

Ryan grabbed his crotch. "You loved it, and now you're gonna *really* miss it." He grinned at Dave. "Give it a week, and this dumb bitch is gonna be begging for it again."

"Hey!" I shouted. "Don't call her that!"

Ryan turned around and faced me. "Or what? You gonna do something about it?"

I stood straighter and put my fists up. "Or… or…or I'll kick your ass."

In hindsight, yeah, I looked and sounded stupid, sure, but I meant what I said.

"That'd be the day." Ryan laughed. "You ain't even half the man your brother was. And he was a pussy."

I stepped forward, my anger blinding, but Ali put out his arm and held me back. If he hadn't, I would've probably lost a good portion of my teeth.

Becca pointed at the door. "Just leave, Ryan."

"If it's what you really want, babe, then I guess I'll let you and the freaks be."

"These *freaks* are cooler than you or Dave will ever be," Becca said.

Chuckling, Ryan pushed the side door and Dave followed him.

As the noise of the outside rushed in, my ears pricked at a sound that did not belong to the storm.

It was a howl.

CHAPTER 13
MOVIES DON'T LIE

THE DISTANT SOUND had made Ryan and Dave stop.

"Uh…did you guys hear that?" Dave asked.

"It was just a dog or something," Ryan said as a flash of lightning lit up the inside of the garage, and the ground shook with ensuing thunder.

"That wasn't a dog," I said.

"Fuck off, Carver. I'm not deaf." Ryan tugged on Dave's shirt. "Let's go, man."

The howl came from the werewolf. But…how did it change if the moon wasn't full?

Then someone outside screamed, the noise high and shrill and all but drowned out by the storm.

"We are so screwed," Ali whispered. "Because

Mr. Thompson was freed, he was able to transform. He is going to want his revenge now."

"Dave, I'm about three seconds away from ditching your fat ass. Move, bro!"

Dave's hand was shaking. It shook only slightly, but it was enough to notice. "Ryan…it sounded like…it sounded like the same howl as that night—"

Ryan threw up his arms. "That's it, I'm out. See ya!"

"You won't make it to your car," I said.

Ryan stopped, inhaled deeply, and turned around. "Say one more word to me, Carver, and see what happens."

"We might make it inside Ali's house. That's our best bet," I continued. "The werewolf'll bust this door down like it's made of cardboard."

"You guys really can't be serious about this werewolf shit," Ryan said.

"Oh, we're serious," Becca said.

Something was knocking against the front of the garage. Through the pelting rain, I heard a painful moan.

I pushed past Ryan and Dave and leaned out the side door, looking into the pool of light cast from the motion sensor. I turned my head to the right and then to the left, seeing nothing.

Until—

"No...*p-please*..."

A pair of bloody hands grabbed the corner of the garage, the nails digging into the siding.

Mr. Thompson's face emerged. One cheek was slashed to ribbons. His right molars showed through the rips in his flesh.

I took a hesitant step toward him, craning my neck for a better view. I could see all the way to his upper chest now, and it was worse off than his face. Deep red grooves were carved into the exposed skin, and the blood, mixed with the falling rain, flowed like a stream.

I reached out for his hand, but when I got about three feet away from him, something jerked him backward, and he let out a gurgling scream.

I did not wait around to see what it was that had taken him.

I turned and shouted to the others. "We gotta go! *Now!*"

―――

I told them to be quiet. Mr. Thompson's death would buy us some time, but if it heard us, the creature would be curious—and its curiosity would kill us.

The thunder and lightning had become more sporadic, but the rain continued to pour.

With me in the lead, we left the garage and went toward Ali's back patio.

Ryan and Dave were the last in line. As I was waving Ali and Becca through the gate, Ryan stopped and looked toward the street. "This is fuckin' crazy," he said. "I'm going to my car."

"Wait, Ryan!" I said as he started down the driveway, but a few feet past the garage, he saw what I assumed to be Mr. Thompson's body and that tripped him up.

I don't know why I did it, I held no sympathy in my heart for Ryan Kensington, but I went after him. Maybe I thought I could be a hero, that I could save his life and he'd like me.

Or maybe I'm just a dumbass.

I raced toward Ryan and grabbed his arm, pulling him toward the house, and that was when I saw the abomination hunched over what was left of Mr. Thompson.

The werewolf, its fur slick with blood and rain, was on all fours, and it had its snout buried at least six inches deep into Mr. Thompson's stomach, ripping and pawing at the man's intestines and guts.

"Holy shit—!" Ryan said.

The werewolf turned its head up in the direction of his voice. It looked at us with eyes as red as the blood coloring its jaws. From between its teeth, a slick pink tube snapped like a rubber band back into Mr. Thompson's belly.

The creature roared.

For some strange reason, I remember thinking, *Grandmother dear, what big teeth you have!*

The sight of a fresh kill now on the werewolf's animalistic brain, it rocked on its haunches and stood.

Even through the storm, I could smell the rotten scent of death and meat on its breath.

I tugged Ryan's arm and, not looking back, dragged him toward Ali's house. This was easy considering he had gone limp.

A large burst of thunder shook the world. With it, the light on the back of the house winked out along with the light on the corner of the road. Neither flickered back on. The power outage was long overdue, but it couldn't have come at a worse time.

"Come on! Come on!" Becca shouted from the open door.

I followed her voice like a beacon as I plowed through the gate and trudged up the few concrete steps that led to the patio.

I felt like I was in a nightmare, the kind where you run and run, pumping your legs as quickly as you can, but you end up getting nowhere. Time was moving in horrible slow motion.

I watched as Becca sighted the werewolf behind me. Her eyes widened and widened until they took up most of her face. "Right there! Watch out!"

I thought, *Grandmother dear, what big eyes you have!*

Ryan was on my heels, somewhat moving on his own, but he must not have noticed the steps, because I heard his muffled exclamation of pain and a dull thud as he fell.

I stopped and tried to help him up, but only managed to grab his hand and get him halfway to his feet before the werewolf pulled him in the opposite direction.

My fear-frenzied brain momentarily refused to see it, I think, but I sensed the werewolf only a few feet away from us.

I reached blindly for something I could use as a

weapon as Ryan screeched in horrible pain. My hand closed around what felt like a steel pole. I raised it, seeing it was nothing but a flimsy meat poker from the nearby grill, and I jabbed it up at the werewolf's face.

My aim wasn't perfect, but I caught the creature in the corner of its open mouth. The metal raked across its teeth and thunked into the soft pink flesh of its gums.

The werewolf yelped and clapped a huge claw-hand to the spot the poker jutted from.

With the creature distracted, this was our chance.

I grabbed Ryan's shirt and pulled with all my might. The stitching twanged and stretched as I got him a few feet away, but then the werewolf grabbed him again.

I tripped and stumbled to my knees. With rain in my eyes, I watched with blurred vision as Ryan was lifted into the air. He kicked and flailed, but the werewolf paid this defiance no mind.

It brought Ryan to its jaws, opened them, and they snapped like a bear trap around his throat.

Blood spurted from his arteries, a red rain that the werewolf lapped at greedily.

"Oh God…" I moaned.

It was too late, I knew. I couldn't help him anymore.

Forcing myself to turn and run as fast as I could toward the back door, I barreled through, knocking into Ali and Dave, and slipping to the floor.

"Close it! Close it!" Becca shouted.

Dave slammed the door shut. He locked it, but I'm sure he knew it wouldn't really help. We all did. "Oh my God," he was saying, his face pressed to the glass. "It's—it's— That can't be real. It got Ryan. Is he—?"

The big guy stood as still as a statue, in shock. We watched as the werewolf, in no hurry now, dragged Ryan's body away into the shadows.

A moment or two of silence passed. Not even the storm interrupted it. Part of my mind thought I could hear the werewolf ripping into Ryan's flesh somewhere out there.

"What do we do now?" Ali whispered. With the sound of his voice came another clap of thunder.

"Call the cops!" Dave said. "Where's your phone?"

Ali pointed into the hall leading to the front door. "But the power's out."

"Shit!" Dave scratched his scalp. Sweat or raindrops (or maybe tears) rolled down his cheeks. "Anyone have a cell?"

I shook my head. So did Ali. "Mine is in the garage," Becca said. "And I'm not going out there to get it." She wiped away tears with the back of her hand.

"We have to keep running, I think," I said. "It'll smash through whatever barricades we put up against it. Now's the time…while it has Ryan."

"Where do we go?" Dave said.

"Away. Far—"

A shadow passed by the back door. I caught a glint of the beast's red eyes before it disappeared around the corner of the house.

I can't confirm this, but I believe it was listening to us. It was listening and it was understanding.

Becca gasped loudly, and Dave jumped as if something had bitten him on the backside.

"It is already back," Ali said.

I waved a hand slowly and whispered, "Everyone move. Get away from the glass." I guided them into the living room. "Ali, are there any weapons in the house?"

He was staring at the front windows. Nothing out there but darkness broken up by the distant lightning strike. On the third flash, we all saw the werewolf's silhouette, stalking around the front yard.

"Weapons," I said again. "We need weapons, Ali!"

A few seconds later, the werewolf thumped into the door with the force of a battering ram and the entire house shook.

I grabbed Ali's sleeve and spun him around. Tears stood out in his eyes. "Ali! Dude! Does your dad have a gun or something? A pocketknife? A fucking baseball bat?!"

"No, no," he said oddly calmly. "It is too late. We are dead, John."

The werewolf howled, as if in response. I heard anger and amusement in that howl, like the creature was toying with us.

"We are doomed, my friends," Ali repeated. Then, quieter to himself, "And I am going to perish in Hell. I should have never stolen the silverware."

"What?"

"I am so sorry. In the eyes of Allah, I have not been a good person—"

I grabbed his shoulders and shook him. "Hey! What did you just say? About the silverware?"

Dave was scooting the couch across the carpet.

He tipped it up and threw it against the door as the werewolf snarled and hit it again.

The hinges groaned, the frame shuddered.

"I stole it, John. From the antique store with the racist shopkeeper. I lied to you…for I was too ashamed. But I swear, it was never my intention to steal. I only stole it *after* he was so rude to me. It was poor judgment. I should have never—"

"Where is the silverware?"

"What? Why?"

The front door quivered with the force of another of the werewolf's blows.

"Where is it!?"

"In—it is in my room, wrapped up under my bed. Why—?"

No time to answer. The door would give in soon.

I rushed to Ali's room on the far west side of the first floor.

Behind me came Becca's startled screams and the splintering of wood. Adrenaline coursing through my veins, I shoved Ali's bed across the room as if it weighed nothing.

Sure enough, in a navy-blue cloth tied in the middle with a golden ribbon, was a set of antique silverware. I picked it up, surprised at how solid it felt, and I rushed into the living room.

The others looked at me. "You guys go. Out the back. Becca, get them to your car and drive!"

"What are you planning on doing?" she asked.

"Creating a distraction."

But that was a lie.

———

Led by Becca, the others filed down the hall and out the back kitchen door. I undid the silk tie and dumped the silverware out, metal ringing through the house.

I found a steak knife. The point was as sharp as it had been the day it was made.

"Hey, you big furry piece of shit! Come and get me!"

The werewolf howled and charged the front door. Wood, hinges, and glass exploded inward.

I shielded my face, feeling it bite into my skin like the stings of dozens of bees but feeling no pain.

The werewolf stood in the threshold, its stature hulking, shoulders rising and falling rapidly with each ragged breath.

Behind, the rain was a solid wall. The storm

clouds had turned hazy and vaguely transparent. Through them burned the bright bulbous moon.

In this light, I could see the werewolf wore a bib of fresh blood beneath its snout. Mostly Ryan and Mr. Thompson's blood, but I saw that more was leaking from the stab wound I gave it earlier.

This brought a satisfying smile to my face that the werewolf seemed to take offense to. It snarled, upper lips rising from its fangs, and we stared at each other.

A car engine turned over outside. The werewolf snapped toward the sound.

"Hey!" I shouted. "Right here!"

Slowly, it turned back toward me and flashed those teeth again.

Grandmother dear, what big…fangs you have?

I will not lie to you. Standing maybe twenty feet away from this supernatural being, trying not to crumble beneath the weight of its menacing red eyes, I felt more fear than I'd thought was possible. And it wasn't fear as I had known it before.

It was an alien fear, one I'd never felt before. The kind of fear that comes to you when you know there is no way out.

I said, "You killed my brother. You killed Owen."

The werewolf tilted its head. A flash of recognition bloomed in its eyes.

As animalistic as it was, I believe the human part, no matter how deeply it might have been buried, was at least somewhat cognizant.

I lowered myself into a crouch, and my muscles went rigid.

The werewolf mimicked my stance, growling as it sprang forward.

I moved quickly to the right, feeling its damp fur brush past my ear. It slid into the hallway, smashing empty picture frames and a mirror off of the wall. Glass shattered and crunched.

I pivoted, still in my half-crouch stance, and raised the silver blade.

To regain its bearings, the werewolf shook like a dog out of water.

The knife was small and the room was dark enough that I don't believe it had noticed it, or maybe it didn't care.

It stood, its long arms stretched in front of it, and advanced, a deep rumbling growing in its chest.

I didn't budge.

A lull in the storm allowed me to hear Becca's car pulling out of the driveway. Good. That was what I wanted.

I bared my teeth. "Come on!"

The creature whipped out its left arm. Despite how prepared I was, I only managed to dodge part of the blow. If I had taken the full force of the hit, I don't think I would be here to tell you this story.

My breath snatched from me, I flew through the broken door and slid across the flooded front lawn.

Somewhere along that short trip, I had lost the silver blade.

Stars danced around the werewolf as it emerged from the darkness of the house. It looked up at the moon and howled. This was a howl of victory.

With me incapacitated, it could now reap the rewards and rip me apart.

I patted the wet grass, searching for the knife, but found nothing besides mud and puddles.

I wasn't about to let this creature kill me lying down. I'd fight. I'd hit the thing, I'd claw its eyes, I'd rip its fur out, I'd bite it back.

I wouldn't give in—because Owen wouldn't have either.

On wobbling legs, I squared up with the werewolf. It regarded me the way a professional boxer might regard a drunk trying to pick a fight on the street.

"Let's go!" I shouted.

The werewolf flashed its fangs and growled as it stepped forward.

I raised my fists the way my older brother had taught me, and I put one foot in front of the other.

The stars still danced in my peripherals, and I was hearing something in my head—not a ringing, but a high-pitched *beeeeep*. At least I thought I was hearing that.

I also thought the moon had grown fuller, because a new brightness had overtaken the front yard.

"MOVE!" someone screamed.

I turned to see not one, but *two* blinding moons. Coming right for me.

That was when I heard the whine of a car engine. The *beeeeep* was not my brain short-circuiting. It was a horn from Becca's car. She was driving right at us, going at least forty, maybe fifty.

I dove to the right, expecting to feel my bones crunch beneath rubber and earth, but I only splashed and rolled in some of the shallow puddles.

The car barreled toward it, and I saw the werewolf attempt a jump. The lawn was so wet, though, it couldn't find enough traction.

What followed was a terrible noise of crumpling

metal and cracking glass, mixing with the screams coming from inside the car.

The werewolf spun over the Honda's roof.

The car fishtailed into the far corner of Ali's house, and the creature hit the grass and tumbled into the driveway, where it lay unmoving.

Pain wracked my body as I went toward the car. I had to make sure my friends—the people who had just saved my life—were okay.

The driver's side door opened. Becca spilled out, her knees splashing in a mud puddle. I bent to help her up. She pushed off me and turned to look at the damage as Ali climbed over the driver's seat.

Dave was trying to get off the backseat floor, but he was dazed and not exactly nimble.

"Holy shit," I said. "Are you guys okay?"

"My mom is gonna be pissed..." Becca said, looking at her busted ride.

"Your mom?" Ali said. He stumbled across the yard, and I grabbed him before he collapsed. His nose was bleeding pretty badly, the blood framing his mouth. "My father is going to absolutely, positively kill me."

"Well, I'll see you in Hell, buddy," Becca said, smiling.

I hugged her, and then I grabbed Ali with my

right arm and pulled him in. They both groaned.

Christ, I can't tell you how relieved I was.

"Dave," Becca called. "You okay?"

"I-I think I pissed myself," Dave's muffled voice answered.

I turned back to Becca and Ali. "I told you guys to get the hell out of here. Drive away—"

"Look out!" Ali shouted.

I spun in time to see the werewolf lunging at us, and it was too late to dodge the attack.

Red eyes flashing, it bowled me over. In a tangled heap we rolled into the car. I could feel its broken bones beneath its flesh, and I swear to you that I could also feel them healing in real-time, as if the thrill of the kill somehow was renewing its strength.

"No!" Ali sprinted at the creature, arms raised.

In one hand, a silver object glinted with moonlight.

The werewolf grabbed my neck and simultaneously swatted Ali away with its free arm, as if he was nothing more than a common house fly.

Launched back the way he had come, Ali gasped, and the blade flung out of his grip, where it rotated and rotated until it landed in the grass hilt-up a few feet away from me.

I reached for it with my right arm. The world was growing dimmer and dimmer as the oxygen was cut from my brain and the werewolf's claws dug into my neck and collar bone.

Inches from my face, the creature roared, spraying bloody spittle and terrible breath. It was done messing around, done playing with its food.

Death was here, and it meant business.

As the darkness was consuming me, I began to picture my brother.

We were back at a park in Pennsylvania. He was smiling as he went through the motions of a reverse layup, a move I absolutely could not get the hang of.

Don't give up, Johnny. Quitting ain't in the Carver DNA. You got this, he was saying.

Reaching, stretching, my fingers closed around cold silver.

You got this, little brother!

And with the little strength I had left, I thrust the blade into the creature's ribs.

It stopped mid-roar, the sound changing to a screeching howl of agony.

All at once, its grip on my throat released, and it fell back, its entire body undulating uncontrollably.

Since I was still gripping the blade's handle, the

falling weight took me with it. Hot blood poured over my knuckles. The werewolf bucked and fought against the burning silver.

I refused to let go.

Hell, I must've held on for at least a minute, until the creature stopped moving. And even then, I wasn't sure I wanted to let go. Doing so might give it another chance to rip my head off. But I eventually did, scooting away and ending up against Becca, who pulled me farther from the monster.

Together, we watched as its face and limbs began to shrink, its hair faded, and its claws and fangs retracted.

Finally, what was left was only a nude woman. Mary, Mr. Thompson's wife.

Her flesh was so pale now, it was almost translucent. Sightless, glassy eyes searched me out as she wriggled the blade free from her ribs, causing more blood to gush from the wound.

She let go of the knife as she focused and raised a hand to my cheek. Her touch was as cold as death.

Then Mary Thompson spoke three words to me.

She said, "I'm so sorry."

AFTER
THE MAN AND HIS DOG

THE DAYS AFTER WERE A BLUR.

Ali, Becca, and I told the police we had suspected Mr. Thompson of murdering my older brother, which had spurred our investigation of him.

Stretching the truth a bit, we said that when the Thompsons found out about our suspicions, they had gone into a terrible rage and tried to kill us. We fought back. It was self-defense.

Pretty self-explanatory. All we did was leave out the part about the werewolf. Dave Rivers chose not to, but we hadn't expected him to. He wasn't one of us. No one believed him anyway.

As it turned out, Mr. Thompson was already suspected of murder across two states in four different Midwestern cities.

I guess he had been sloppy when cleaning up some of his wife's messes. Local police departments had coordinated across their respective jurisdictions and gathered enough evidence to feel confident in charging him before all of the madness went down that June night.

Whether he would've gone to prison for the murders was unknown, and still is to this day, because the very beast he had been trying to protect was the same beast that had ripped him open.

What followed were a lot of interviews with the Pickwick PD, and even more with the state police and, I think, the FBI.

All three of us stuck to our guns, though. Because the evidence of the Thompsons' attack was obvious and we were just "dumb teenagers," as the Pickwick police chief had so lovingly put it, they seemed to believe us.

Ali's father was not pissed about anything that happened, surprisingly. I thought he would maybe drag Ali and his brother back to Oman, but he seemed to really love the fact that his son had helped stop a serial killer. In his eyes, Ali was one step closer to an American hero.

In town, the three of us were treated like royalty. The mayor even gave us a key to the city.

Not even the racist dickbag whose stolen silverware had wound up killing the werewolf said anything bad of Ali again. In fact, he had approached him one day and shook his hand, thanking him.

I've heard that those who experience trauma together and live to tell about it are bonded for life. Maybe that was the case between Ali, Becca, and myself, but as June became July and July became August, I saw less and less of them.

Ali had gone back to Oman for a few weeks to visit with his mother and the rest of his family over there.

Becca, in an attempt to distract herself from the horrors of what we saw, put her head down and found a second job as a waitress at some Italian place in Downtown Akron.

As a trio, we had met only once more that summer to film the last scenes of *Creature*, but the fun we had had during the earlier sessions was gone.

It was all business, which I didn't mind for the sake of finishing the movie, but I missed how it was before we fought the werewolf.

Because after that, life seemed…*heavier*, I guess.

———

The last filming session happened sometime in mid-August, on a scorching hot evening.

My mother never turned on the central air conditioning in the summer unless absolutely necessary, but I remember it blasting that whole week. It hummed blissfully in the cool downstairs bathroom, where Becca and I were crammed together near the sink.

She was studying herself in the mirror, covered in fake blood and slime from her final battle with the creature. I stood diagonally to her left so my reflection wouldn't be visible.

"Like this?" she asked me, picking at the scabby makeup wound Ali had applied on her neck.

"Yeah, yeah," I said. "That's pretty good. Hold it there for a second…and—"

There was a knock at the front door. Ali, in my kitchen washing his hands of the monster makeup, yelled, "John! You have a visitor!"

"I'm coming. Hold on."

I set my camera down on the closed toilet and nodded at Becca. "Probably the mailman dropping off a package or something. I'll be right back."

"All right," she said.

The person knocked again, this time more urgently.

Shaking my head, slightly annoyed at the disruption, I went toward the front door but stopped when I saw the silhouettes of two figures through the sheer curtains.

"No way," I said.

Ali's footsteps came up behind me. "Who is it?"

I shushed him, grabbing his arm and ducking out of view from the windows. Then I motioned back toward the bathroom, where I intended to hide until the man and his dog were gone.

As I crawled down the hall, the man's gruff voice said, "I see you, Carver!"

"And dogs basically have supersonic hearing," said another voice.

"Do you hear them?" I asked Ali. "Please tell me you don't."

Since my run-in with the man in the park a couple of months ago, I had convinced myself that I had imagined the whole experience, that maybe I had dozed off on the bench in the shade of the big oak and dreamt it all.

This seemed plausible enough until I saw who was standing on the other side of my front door. The man and the strange inverted Dalmatian were like nightmares come alive.

"Who are they?" Ali asked.

"Did you hear the dog? It talked."

Ali narrowed his eyes. "The dog talked? What? I heard two men."

"Listen, Carver," the man said, "I just wanna talk to you real quick. You don't gotta worry about getting hurt."

Rising to a half-crouch, I cleared my throat and said, "Go away. Please."

Becca had come out of the bathroom and was leaning around the corner, head cocked. Ali shrugged at her.

"We wanna make you an offer, Carver. You and your friends."

I squinted. "What's the offer?".

"Open the door, please. I know your ma probably told you not to open the door for strangers, but trust me, we ain't gonna hurt—"

"He might open the door if you'd stop acting like a dick," the other voice said…the voice of the *dog*.

The man sighed. "Carver, I'm sorry. All right? It's been a rough few weeks. That don't excuse my rudeness, I know. Just let me make my offer and then we'll be on our way."

"Tell him about the money," the dog said.

Another sigh left the man, this one heavier.

"Yeah, there's money. Good money for all of you, if you're as good at hunting as the Order thinks you are."

"Shit," Becca said. "John, open the door."

"This is exactly how people get murdered, you know," I said to her, frowning.

"Also how people miss out on opportunities," she countered. "But"—she changed to a whisper—"we, like, slayed a werewolf. We're indestructible."

"Usually I am the voice of reason," Ali said. "But I do agree with Becca there. We are indestructible."

"So I should open the door?" I said.

"You should open the door!" the man said.

I shook my head at my friends as I went down the hall to the foyer and unlocked the deadbolt and took off the chain. "I'm gonna regret this, I can already feel it."

Slowly, I opened the door.

There, in almost the same raggedy clothes I had seen him in at the park all those weeks ago, was the man and the dog with black fur and white spots.

The man offered his hand. I looked at it for a moment before he got the message and dropped it.

"Yeah, okay, well, my name's Zeke. Nice to officially meet you." He stepped inside, pushing past us. "Can we come in? Okay, good."

The dog trailed after him.

"Whoa!" Becca said from over my shoulder. "Cute pup."

"You aren't too bad yourself," the second voice replied. "Though I could do without all the fake blood. Smells sour."

Becca froze and looked up at the man. "You didn't say that, did you?"

"Nope. That was me," the dog said. It spoke without moving its lips, its voice filling our heads in some crazy telepathic way. "Down here."

"That—that dog just spoke," Ali said.

"Yeah," the man named Zeke said. "You'll probably never get used to that."

This was good. It meant I wasn't insane after all —but also...*what the fuck?*

Becca, still staring at the dog, who seemed to be smiling, sat on the bench by the shoes.

"I'm no puppy either. I'm not even a dog," the dog said. "I *was* a dog. Now I'm dead. You can call me Ziggy."

"You're a ghost dog?" I said breathlessly.

"Something like that," Ziggy replied.

Okay, maybe I was insane. And again—*what the fuck?*

Zeke put his hands on his hips and looked around as he walked into the living room. "Nice place you got here." He sat on the couch and kicked his feet up.

"Where's your manners, you ass?" Ziggy said as he nudged the man's feet back to the floor with his muzzle.

"Yeah, yeah," Zeke grumbled. He straightened and cleared his throat.

I helped Becca up and then pulled Ali out of the foyer into the living room to join the strangers.

"Can someone please tell us what the hell is going on?" I said.

"That would be Old Stick-Up-His-Ass's job here." Ziggy pointed his snout at the man.

"The dog is talking," Ali said, his lips trembling.

Zeke nodded. "Yeah, kid, we established that already."

"The d-dog is talking."

The man rolled his eyes. "Fried his brain, I guess. That happens. Oh well. Okay, yeah, back to business." He dug a hand into the inside pocket of his dark jacket and pulled out a card.

On the back of it was the same symbol the man had tattooed on his left hand. The curled tentacles.

He read from it. "'Jonathan Dell Carver, Ali Bu Ali Al-Kareem, and Rebecca Faye Tanner, you have been invited to formally partake in an apprenticeship with The Order of the Octopus. Upon completion of three-hundred hours on the—blah…blah…blah, passing of the Trials…blah, blah, blah—a permanent position will be offered.'" The man waved his tattooed hand. "Christ, they really need to get a better writer for these things."

"I have no idea what is going on," I said.

Ziggy jumped soundlessly onto the chair and pawed the throw pillow until it was suitably comfortable, then he plopped down.

"You're getting offered a job," the dog said. "The Order is going bananas over you guys. It's not every day a group of teenagers takes out a full-grown werewolf."

"Yeah, yeah, whatever," Zeke said.

"They're calling you prodigies," Ziggy went on.

"They're more like thieves," Zeke mumbled.

"Who did your job for you," Ziggy said. "You should be thanking them."

"You're lucky you're already dead, Zig."

"Ooh, I'm so scared."

I interrupted their banter. "What Order?"

"The Order of the Octopus," Ziggy answered. "Kind of a secret organization. Kind of a big deal. We protect the world from things that go bump in the night."

"We try to, at least," Zeke said. "Listen, kid, I'm just the messenger. Only reason I'm here is so I don't get suspended without pay. I'll tell you this, though, the job ain't easy. You think going up against a full-grown werewolf is hard? Wait until you stumble across a vamp nest."

"Vampires?" Becca said. "This is crazy. You gotta be joking—wait…never mind." She sighed. "The dog's talking, and I've seen a real live werewolf. Nothing's impossible anymore."

"Exactly," Zeke said, getting up. "But yeah, the information's on the card." He tossed it on the coffee table. "Join us or don't. I don't give a shit." He snapped his fingers. "C'mon, Zig, let's get out of this pisshole of a town."

"So testy," Ziggy said. "Just ignore him. Look into it, though. We could use you in the Order. Bobby Dylan knew it back in '65 when he said the times are a-changing. World's growing darker."

Ziggy hopped off the couch, and rather than walk around the coffee table, the Dalmatian faded to an almost transparent version of itself and went *through* it.

I watched with wide eyes, unable to find any words. A moment later, the front door opened and closed.

We were left standing there, staring in disbelief.

Becca picked up the card. "Yeah, well, count me out. No amount of money could get me in the same room with a werewolf ever again."

All Ali said was, "The dog…the dog was talking."

I patted him on the back. Becca handed me the card. I snorted and said, "Yeah, no way."

But I kept the card.

Fighting monsters for money? I'll admit, I was curious.

"Let's finish this damn movie," Becca said, going back to the bathroom.

Sure, we had faced and beaten a werewolf, but I still don't understand how we were able to go back to normal after meeting a talking ghost dog and learning about a secret order that fought *"things that went bump in the night."*

Yet…we did.

And the summer went on.

Near the end of August, Becca struck out west for Hollywood, chasing her dream of becoming a famous actress.

Last I had heard she was auditioning for any and everything while taking acting classes somewhere in Los Angeles.

On the day she left, Becca had kissed me again on the cheek, and again I had felt like I was floating.

I didn't hear much from her for the rest of the summer, but when the Harvest Festival came around she surprised Ali and I by showing up in the front row of the viewing tent.

"You're back!" I said, rushing over to her. Ali and I wrapped her up in a big hug.

"Well, duh," she said. "I wouldn't miss this. After all, I'm the star of the movie, aren't I?"

Speaking of *Creature*, I didn't get a chance to finish it the way I had envisioned. But after some rushed edits, Ali and I managed to make it into a somewhat coherent story.

Instead of a crowd-pleaser, I took a chance and opted for the ambiguous ending. Becca's character defeats the monster, but in the process is possibly infected by it.

The last scene is the one we were working on when we were visited by the Order of the Octopus. It is of Becca looking in the mirror and bringing a finger to a spot below her jawline where the skin has turned slightly greenish.

The question I wanted to ask was this: Had she defeated the monster only to become one herself?

Out of the seven entries in the Harvest Festival's Short Film Contest, *Creature* placed fourth.

I was okay with that. And even though I never pursued a career in film-making, I still think back to that last shot of Becca touching her discolored throat.

After all these years, after all I've been through, after all the monsters I've faced and defeated—yes, stories for another time—I often wonder the same thing.

Have I become a monster?

ABOUT THE AUTHOR

Flint Maxwell lives in Ohio with his beautiful wife, his son and daughter, and their four furry best friends.

Made in United States
Orlando, FL
22 June 2023